The Damsel

*Grofield novels
by Donald E. Westlake,
writing as Richard Stark*

The Damsel

The Dame

The Blackbird

Lemons Never Lie

The Damsel

A Grofield Novel

Donald E. Westlake

writing as Richard Stark

A Foul Play Press Book

The Countryman Press, Inc.
Woodstock, Vermont

This edition first published in 1990 by Foul Play Press, an imprint of The
Countryman Press, Inc., Woodstock, Vermont 05091.

ISBN 0-88150-156-5

Printed in the United States of America

10 9 8 7 6 5 4 3 2

To LARRY,

in lieu of

CONTENTS

PART ONE

1

GROFIELD OPENED his right eye, and there was a girl climbing in the window. He closed that eye, opened the left, and she was still there. Gray skirt, blue sweater, blond hair, and long tanned legs straddling the windowsill.

But this room was on the fifth floor of the hotel. There was nothing outside that window but air and a poor view of Mexico City.

Grofield's room was in semidarkness, because he'd been taking an after-lunch snooze. The girl obviously thought the place was empty, and once she was inside she headed straight for the door.

Grofield lifted his head and said, "If you're my fairy god-mother, I want my back scratched."

She jumped a foot, landed like a cat, and backed away to the far wall, staring at him. In the dimness her eyes looked as white as stars, gleaming with panic.

Grofield hadn't expected that big a reaction. He tried to calm her, reassure her, saying, "I mean it. I'm stuck in this bed and my back itches like crazy. If you've got a minute while you're pass-ing through, you could scratch it for me."

She said, "Are you one of them?" Her voice was scratchy with panic.

"That depends. Sometimes I'm one of them and other times it doesn't seem worth the effort. I haven't been one of them lately because I haven't been well."

The glitter was slowly fading from her eyes. In a more human voice she said, "What are you talking about?"

"Be damned if I know. Are we supposed to be talking about something?" He tried to sit up, but the wound in his back gave him a twinge. He grimaced and shook his head. "It gets worse," he said. "Before it gets better, it gets worse."

She came one hesitant step away from the wall. "You're hurt?"

"Nothing, *mon capitaine*, a flesh wound merely. If only some Florence Nightingale would scratch my back, my recovery would be complete."

"I'll trust you," she said, taking another step closer to the bed. "God knows, I have to trust somebody."

"You wouldn't talk like that if I had full use of my faculties."

All at once she looked at the ceiling, as though afraid it might fall, and then again at Grofield. "Will you help me?"

"Will you scratch my back?"

Impatience was now replacing her departed panic. "This is serious!" she said. "A matter of life and death!"

"There is no such thing, but I tell you what. You scratch my back, I'll save your life. Is it a deal?"

She said, "If you'll let me stay here. For a day or two, just till it's safe."

Grofield smiled. "I've been lying in this bed for days," he said. "I've got nobody to talk to, nothing to read, nothing to do. From time to time I get up and totter to the bathroom and totter back again. When I wake up from a nap, as now, my back is stiff where it was hurt and itches everywhere else. Three times a day the assistant desk clerk, an oily young man with a thick moustache and an offensive smile, brings me a tray of garbage and tells me it's food and I eat it. Darling, if you will sometimes talk to me and at other times scratch my back, you can stay here forever. In fact, I'll pay you to stay here forever."

All at once she smiled. "I like you," she said. "I like your attitude."

"You'll love my back."

She came the rest of the way over to the bed. "Can you sit up?"

"Not yet. Every time I wake up, I'm too stiff to move. Maybe I can roll over."

"I'll help."

He gave her his right hand. She tugged and he squirmed and soon he was over on his face, the covers all messed up. She said, "Aren't you wearing *any*thing?"

"I'm wearing the whole bed," he said into the pillow. "Isn't that enough?"

She rearranged the covers, pulling them back up to his waist. "It is now. What's this bandage for?"

"My wound."

She touched it, tentatively. His back was taped and bandaged high on the left side, near the shoulder blade. "What sort of wound?"

"Cupid's arrow. I gazed into the smoky eyes of a lovely *señorita*, and the next thing I knew, Cupid gave me the shaft."

"You're in trouble, too," she said.

"Not a bit of it. I have the world on a string." He squirmed a bit. "Would you start scratching? Mostly around the bandage."

She started scratching. "Bandages should be changed, you know."

"A contortionist I'm not."

She scratched his back in long, easy strokes. "You say you're not in trouble," she said thoughtfully. "You've been wounded some way—"

"Arrow."

"Some way. You're lying here all alone, you obviously don't want a doctor looking at you, you aren't leaving the room at all and—oh!"

"Oh? Keep scratching."

"Sorry. I just realized what it must be."

"What what must be?"

"Your wound. It's a gunshot wound, isn't it? That's why you don't want to let a doctor see it."

"Now let's talk about you."

She said, "The police are looking for you, I bet."

Grofield considered his answer. She didn't seem particularly displeased at the thought of his being wanted by the police, and she was in any case in some kind of a jam herself that evidently didn't include phoning the cops. So it was time to give her a story

5

that would satisfy her and would also keep her quiet later on, in case her own troubles got her mixed up with the law. Grofield took a deep breath and said, "You're right. The police *are* looking for me."

"I thought so. What did you do?"

"I followed Love," he told her, "wherever it would lead me."

"You're going off into that crazy talk again," she said.

"No, I'm not. It's the truth. I was living in New York, and there I met a woman. A woman as beautiful as she was fickle, as amorous as she was treacherous. She was a Castilian from Mexico City, alabaster skin and ebony hair, married to a man twenty years older than herself, but a powerful political figure in this country. This woman—I dare not speak her name—she and I had a whirlwind affair while she was in New York, and when she returned to Mexico I couldn't help myself, I followed her. We couldn't keep away from one another, and in our passion we were careless."

"He caught you," she said. She sounded just a bit breathless.

Grofield smiled into the pillow. Women prefer to believe a romance every time, and this one was no exception. "You've guessed it," he said. "He returned home unexpectedly, we—"

"In his *house?* What were you, crazy?"

"An interesting comment. We must discuss *your* past very soon."

"Never mind that," she said, and playfully slapped him between the shoulder blades. "Tell me what happened."

"It's simply told. He came in, we were in bed, he ran to the dresser and pulled out a gun. I went racing down the hallway, my clothes in my arms, and he shot me in the back as I was going out the front door. I managed to get to a friend of mine, someone I knew from New York who was visiting down here, and he got me to a doctor and then checked me into this hotel. But then his vacation was up and he had to go back to the States. And now it seems the husband has sworn out a warrant against me for burglary and assault, so the Mexico City police are after me."

She stopped scratching and said, "What are you going to do?"

"Don't stop. I don't know what I'll do. My tourist visa, all my papers, I left behind in my lady's bedroom. My friend lent me some money before he left, but once it's gone, I don't know. I've just been lying here, waiting to get better. Once I'm healthy again, I can decide what to do next."

"Maybe you can take refuge in the American Embassy."

"Hardly. I'm not wanted for political reasons. As far as the Mexico City police are concerned, I'm nothing but a common burglar, a housebreaker."

"Well," she said, "misery loves company, so we ought to get along just fine."

She'd swallowed the story whole. Grofield grinned at the pillow and said, "What about you? What brought you climbing through my window just in time to scratch my back?"

"Oh, it's a long story," she said. "It really doesn't matter."

"Fair's fair. I told you my troubles, now you tell me yours."

"Well . . . I'm just afraid I'll start crying again if I talk about it."

Grofield twisted half-around in the bed and looked up over his hurt shoulder at her. She did look sad, very small-girlish. "You'll feel better if you talk it out," he said. It was the kind of bushwah line that seemed appropriate under the circumstances, just as the tale of the cuckolded politico had seemed the appropriate kind of bushwah story to tell.

It apparently worked, because she said, "All right, I will. I owe you that much."

Grofield relaxed again, facing front, resting his cheek on the pillow.

The girl said, "My troubles are all about love, too, but a different kind of love from yours." She sounded very puritanical, very disapproving, when she said that. "I love a boy who has no money at all," she said, "and my aunt wants me to marry a man I can't stand."

Could that possibly be legit? Grofield turned his head and looked up at her again, and her face was as guileless as a choir boy's. "Things like that don't happen," he said.

"You may think it's funny," she said, and now her lip had

7

started to tremble, "and I don't blame you if you laugh, but after all, it's my whole life."

"All right, all right. I'm not laughing." Grofield subsided, giving her the benefit of the doubt. After all, even clichés come true every once in a while.

"I know it sounds silly," she said. She'd stopped scratching his back now and was massaging it instead, which felt even better. "I'm so young and all, I suppose I sound foolish. But I *do* love Tom, and I *don't* love Brad, and that's all there is to it!"

"I'm for you," Grofield said. He was getting sleepy again.

"My aunt took me away on this so-called vacation," she went on, "to get me away from Tom. And now Brad's down here, too, and my aunt is talking about us getting married right away, right here in Mexico City, and I absolutely refuse to do it. It got so bad, my aunt locked me in my room, because she knows all I want to do is get back home and be with Tom."

"So you tied sheets together," Grofield said drowsily, "and climbed down them to my window."

"Yes."

"But the sheets are still there, hanging out the window. Your aunt will look down, and she'll know you're here."

"She won't believe I stayed here. That's why I want to stay, don't you see? She'll call the police and everything, hire private detectives, have the airport watched, and all the rest of it. She and Brad both. But if I wait here a day or two until they're sure I've slipped out of their grasp, then they'll stop looking so hard and I'll be able to get away. Also, I'll have to wire Tom to send me some money."

"I thought he was broke."

"He can get some, enough for plane fare for me."

"Good for Tom." Grofield closed his eyes and gave himself up to the pleasure of having his back massaged. "Stouthearted Tom," he mumbled, "he's true-blue."

"He's the man I'm going to marry," she said, sounding young and delicious and determined.

"Right."

"You go to sleep if you want," she said. "Sleep's what you need now, while you recuperate."

"Oh, no," he said. "No, no, I won't be sleeping. I just woke up." Besides, something was bothering him. Wasn't there something she'd said, something when she'd just come in, something . . ." Something that didn't connect with this Tom-Brad-aunt story, something . . .

"Go on and sleep," she said soothingly. "Rest. Relax. Sleep. I'll be here."

Grofield was as relaxed as a puddle of ketchup, but still that something was tugging at his brain, until all at once he thought: *Are you one of them?*

That was it, that was what she'd said. Are you one of them, that was the sentence. It didn't make any sense with the aunt story, not a bit of sense. He ought to ask her about that, but somehow speech would take too much effort. In fact, thinking was taking too much effort. Not that he was going to sleep, it was just—

He opened his eyes and knew at once he'd been sleeping, but he had no idea for how long. A minute? Five hours?

He was lying on his back now, staring up at the ceiling. He was abruptly, electrically, immediately awake, as though some sudden noise had jolted him from sleep.

He looked around the room, raising his head from the pillow, and saw the girl standing at the foot of the bed. She had taken his suitcase from the closet, had put it on the rack at the foot of the bed, and had opened it. It stood open now, and she stood on the other side of it, looking at him.

He said, "What have you done?"

"I was going to hang your clothes up," she said. "I saw your suitcase on the closet floor, and nothing on the hangers at all, so I thought I'd empty the suitcase, let your clothes hang their wrinkles out."

"You're too kind," Grofield said bitterly.

She reached down into the suitcase and held up two handfuls of money, American currency. "Maybe you'd better think of a new story to tell," she said.

2

GROFIELD SAID, "I wear money."

"That isn't funny," she said. "That isn't at all funny." She threw the double handful of bills back into the suitcase.

"I thought it was pretty humorous," Grofield said. "Not a knee-slapper maybe, but surely worth at least a chuckle, a little smile, a—"

"Oh, stop it. You had me going, I admit it, you had me feeling sorry for you, thinking you had this fantastic romantic adventure, and now you're in desperate trouble, all for love, and all the rest of that malarkey."

"I was rather fond of that story, myself," Grofield admitted.

"Well, you'd better try for a better one," she said.

Grofield considered, and wondered if it was time for the truth. Sometimes the best way to hide the truth is to tell it at a time when your listener expects a lie—a variant on *The Purloined Letter*. Having already rejected the truth as a lie, the listener is later more likely to misinterpret any inadvertent slips or unforeseen clues that might arise.

This seemed like such a moment, so Grofield smiled a cunning smile and said, "I stole it."

"I've already guessed that part of it. The question is, where?"

"From a gambling casino on an island off the coast of Texas. You see, I'm an actor, and it's impossible to make ends meet these days as an actor in the legitimate theater. Unless you're willing to peddle your integrity to the movie and television people, there's nothing for it—"

"What on earth," she said, "are you talking about?"

"Acting," he said. "Do you realize that in my peak year so far I earned a miserable thirty-seven hundred dollars from acting?"

"What about this money here?" she demanded, pointing at the suitcase.

"Sixty-three thousand dollars. A bunch of us knocked over that gambling casino, and that's my share."

"Gambling casino," she said contemptuously. "Off the coast of Texas. So how do you wind up here?"

"It's a long story," he said.

"By the time you're done making it up," she said, "I suppose it will be. The last story you were Casanova, this time you're Robin Hood. Who are you going to be next time, Flash Gordon?"

"You mean you don't believe me?"

"Of course not," she said.

Grofield hid a grin with a look of mock distress. The fact was, everything he'd just told her was true. He really was an actor, and a moderately good one, tall and lean and darkly handsome, usually cast as the evil brother or weak son or charming knave. But his attitude toward movies and television kept him limited to the poverty-stricken arena of legitimate theater. Happily, he had an outside source of income, a second profession, from which he made a great deal of money indeed.

He was a thief. In company with small groups of other professionals like himself, he took large amounts of money from institutions, never from individuals. Banks, armored cars, jewelry stores, factories, these were the targets. Once or twice a year he went in on a job like that, and made enough to support himself in style while working as an actor.

He'd gotten into this second profession almost by accident, seven years before. He'd been in summer stock, with a repertory company in Pennsylvania. The company was going broke, and four of the guys started talking, as a gag at first, about "knocking over a liquor store or a gas station." Gradually it became less a gag and more specific; a supermarket in a suburban area forty miles away. And then it wasn't a gag at all, and they were actually doing it, wearing masks, toting prop guns loaded with blanks, traveling in an old Chevy with mud smeared on the plates, all of them feeling the butterflies they knew well as stage fright. They got forty-three hundred dollars, and they weren't caught.

For a year after that, Grofield went back to starving the honest, safe way, and never talked about the supermarket robbery at all. But one time, trading anecdotes with an old buddy from Army days, Grofield told him what had happened, and the guy laughed and offered Grofield a spot driving the car in a jewelry-store heist. It turned out he was a pro at this sort of thing.

That was number two. By number three, Grofield was a pro himself.

This last one, the sixty-three thousand in the suitcase, had been job number twelve, and the damnedest one of the lot. It had been set up by a guy named Parker, with whom Grofield had worked a couple of times in the past. Off the Texas coast there really was an island with a gambling casino on it. The syndicate boys on the mainland were upset about this casino, since they didn't own it and couldn't control it, so they'd financed Parker to rob the place on condition he and his partners wreck it while there. Parker had brought in Grofield and a couple of other guys, and then the job had gotten complicated. By the time it was over, Parker and Grofield were the only ones left, down in Mexico City with the proceeds of the job, Grofield with a bullet in his back. Parker had fixed him up first with a doctor and second with a hotel room, had split the money in half, and had gone back with his half to the States, leaving Grofield to recuperate on his own time.

A boring interval, until now. But now he had this girl to focus his interest on, and to bamboozle. Having told her a cutdown version of the truth in such a way as to convince her it was a lie, he now switched stories abruptly, making a sandwich of lies with the truth hidden away in the middle. "I don't suppose there's any reason you should believe me," he said ruefully.

"Right as rain," she said.

"But believe me," he said, "I'm only trying to protect you."

"Protect me? What's that supposed to mean?"

"If I were to tell you the truth," he said, "you'd be in as much danger as I am. The men who shot me play for keeps. If they thought you knew what was going on, they'd kill you as quick as look at you. We're safe now, because they don't know I'm here, but who knows what could happen tomorrow, or the next day?"

"What are you up to now?" she demanded.

"Please believe me—"

"I wouldn't believe you on a stack of Bibles."

He sighed. "It's better that way, better you don't know."

"Oh, stop—"

A sudden knocking at the door shut her up as though she'd been switched off. She got wide-eyed again, with a return of her earlier panic, and whispered shrilly, "It's them! They're looking for me!"

Grofield pointed at the window. "Up the sheet," he whispered. "I'll play dumb."

She nodded and ran to the window.

There was more knocking at the door, and a voice called in an American accent, "Hey! Anybody home in there?"

Grofield called, "Just a second, just a second." The girl was on her way out the window, in a swirl of gray skirt and tanned legs. Grofield shouted, "The door's unlocked. Come in."

The door swung violently open and bounced against the wall. Three of them came in, stocky hoods with thick faces and worried expressions. They looked forty ways at once and one of them came over to stand beside the bed, look down at Grofield, and say, "You seen a girl in here?"

"In here? Only in my dreams, friend."

"Whadaya doin, layin there? You drunk?"

"Sick. I got gored by a bull."

"Tough. Get ya in the privates?"

"Good God, no. My back, by the shoulder."

He laughed. "You was goin the other way."

"Sane men do."

The other two meantime had searched the room. It hadn't taken long. They opened the closet and bathroom doors, glanced inside, shut the doors again, then looked behind the armchair and under the bed and that was that. One of them went over to the window and leaned out and looked up, and Grofield hoped the girl had had sense enough to go all the way up and back into the room upstairs, and haul the sheet in after her. Apparently she had, because the guy brought his head back in, looked at the one who talked, and shook his head.

The talker looked back to Grofield. "The reason we're here," he said, "is because there's a crazy dame loose."

"A crazy dame?"

"Yeah. You know, coo-coo." He made circles beside his head.

Grofield nodded. "Got it," he said. "Off her wonk, you mean."

"That's it. We're supposed to deliver her to her father in South America, only she got away from us."

"South America," said Grofield.

"She got away from us," the guy repeated, meaning that was the part of the sentence he wanted Grofield to think about. "She hung a sheet out the window. We figure she came down the sheet, in your window here, and out of the place. You been right here all day?"

"Right here," said Grofield. "Only I've been asleep most of the time."

"How come when we knocked you said just a second, just a second? What were you doin?"

"Coming back to bed. I'd just been to the head."

"So what?"

Grofield looked coy. "Underneath here," he said, "I'm all nudey."

"Is that right?"

"That's right."

"So you figure she must of gone through the room while you were asleep."

"If she came through, it was while I was asleep. I haven't seen anybody since lunch, and that was the desk clerk when he brought the food up."

"You wouldn't of seen this girl, and she told you a crazy persecution-complex story, and you believed it, would you?"

"Not me."

"Yeah." The guy reached out all at once and yanked the covers off Grofield, who shouted, "Hey!"

"That's okay," said the guy. "Just checkin." Satisfied, he flipped the covers back up over Grofield again. "Take care of yourself," he said, and to the other two, "Come on, boys."

"I don't think I liked that," Grofield said.

One of them stopped by his suitcase, which was closed again but still out in plain sight. He seemed as though he might be thinking about opening it, just out of idle curiosity. Grofield said, loudly, "I think you three are a bunch of bastards, if you want to know."

The two silent ones both looked mad, but the talker laughed and said, "That's okay, we don't mind. See you around."

At least the other one wasn't thinking about the suitcase anymore. All three of them walked over to the door, and Grofield watched them with a face that showed nothing but outrage.

At the door, the talker turned and said, "Keep away from the bulls, buddy." He laughed, and followed the other two out, and shut the door behind him.

"Ha, ha," said Grofield sardonically. He shifted position till he could use his right arm to lever himself up, and managed to get into a sitting position by the time those long tanned legs came swinging in the window again.

The rest of the girl followed, landing gracefully on hands and knees and popping right up again. "I want to thank you," she said.

Grofield said, "I don't like those guys."

"They're dreadful, terrible, awful."

"On the other hand," Grofield went on, "I don't think I like you a hell of a lot either."

"Me? Why, what did I do?"

"Just answer me one thing. Which one of those three was your aunt?"

She blushed. "Oh," she said. "The lie, you mean."

"The lie, I mean, right. Your aunt, and Brad, and Tom, that sterling cast of characters."

She made embarrassed faces, embarrassed gestures. "I didn't know what to do, what to say. I wasn't sure I could trust you."

"You're getting a whopper ready," he said, "I can tell the signs."

"No, I'm not. Really."

"Cross your heart, honey. You forgot to cross your heart."

"Now, don't be nasty," she said. "Besides, what about you? You told a pretty big whopper yourself."

"Only to protect you, only to keep you from getting in even worse trouble than you already are."

"Oh, if you think I believe that—"

"Why not? What's wrong with it?"

"I wouldn't," she told him, "I wouldn't believe a word you said to me."

"Honey, I feel exactly the same way about you."

They faced each other, both somewhat irritated, both displaying more irritation than they felt, both thinking desperately. Until Grofield, seeing how identical they were being, suddenly burst out laughing, and a second later she started laughing too. She sat down on the edge of the bed and laughed, and Grofield leaned forward over his knees and laughed, and they kept on that way a while and gradually subsided into friendly silence.

Grofield finally broke it, saying, "I could use a drink. How about you?"

"Desperately."

"I'll get us a bottle and some ice," Grofield suggested, and reached for the phone.

"Don't let anybody know I'm here!"

"Don't worry about a thing. The desk clerk is madly in love with my money. You hungry?"

"Starved, as a matter of fact. Excitement always makes me hungry."

"The life you live, I'm surprised you're not fat as a horse."

"What do you know about the life I live?"

"It includes those three aunties of yours, doesn't it? Any life that includes that trio is bound to be exciting. And probably short." Grofield picked up the phone. "I'll get us food," he said.

3

"Aaahh," she said in contentment, and smiled, and patted her lips with the napkin, and pushed the tray away across the table. "That was good."

"I could use a fresh drink," Grofield told her. "And then we'll talk."

"Right. Then we'll talk."

In the last half hour, since he'd made the call for food and drink, they'd said practically nothing to one another, both accepting this as a sort of time-out. She'd insisted on hiding in the closet while the desk clerk, grinning evilly beneath his moustache, brought in the huge tray of food, and since then she'd sat demurely at the writing table across the room, packing it in like an infantryman after a forty-mile hike.

Now she got to her feet, gathered up their two glasses, took them over to the bottle of scotch and the ice bucket on the dresser, and made fresh drinks. She came back and sat down on the edge of the bed, handed Grofield his glass, and said, "Who goes first?"

"Names first," he said. "We might as well have something to call one another. My name's Grofield, Alan Grofield, and that's straight."

"Hello, Alan Grofield. I'm Ellen Marie Fitzgerald, and that's also straight."

"It sounds straight enough. What do they call you?"

"Elly, mostly."

Grofield practiced raising his left arm. It was feeling better and better, and was only really bad immediately after sleep. "Let me," he said, "let me run down what I know about you, Ellen Marie, and then you see if you can tell a straight story to fill in the blank spaces."

She smiled, looking pert, and said, "I love to be the center of attention."

"The hell you do. That Gale Storm bit doesn't suit you, honey."

Her smile got a bit more honest. "Circumstances are against me," she said. "But go ahead, tell me my story."

"Right. You're a young girl, good-looking, unmarried, from the northeastern part of the United States. A city, somewhere between Washington and Boston, but probably neither of those. Maybe New York, but I'll take a stab at Philadelphia. Okay so far?"

Her smile had faltered, and now was turning sour. "Are you very clever," she asked him, "or are you a part of this somehow? Do you already know everything?"

"I knew nothing," he told her, "until you came in my window. And *that's* straight. Surely it shouldn't have been that tough to tell you were a big-city girl from the northeast. I doubted it was New York, because when I told you I came from New York you didn't ask me what part. People always ask strangers from the same city what part of the city they live in. Boston and Washington both would probably have left some trace of accent in your speech, and you have none, so that left Philadelphia."

"And Baltimore," she said. "And Wilmington. And Trenton. And Buffalo. And Cleveland."

He shook his head. "*Big* city. And not Baltimore because Baltimore is Pittsburgh, and you aren't from Pittsburgh."

She laughed and clapped her hands, a return to the girl-child style. "You're wonderful," she said. "You're delightful. I believe you now, you looked at me and guessed I came from Philadelphia."

"But not your three aunties," Grofield said, gesturing at the door. "They're New York, the three of them, and they're professional hoods, and your background shouldn't cross theirs anywhere. So. A rich girl from Philadelphia is being held prisoner by three New York hoods in a respectable middle-income hotel in Mexico City. Fine so far?"

"As nicely put as anything I've ever heard. And I know what *you* do for a living. You write those paragraphs called 'The Story So Far' in front of serial chapters in the magazines."

Grofield grinned. "My secret is out. But don't tell anybody."

"I promise. Are you done with me?"

"Not quite. You escaped from the hoods, but you didn't call the cops, which means it isn't a straight kidnapping job. You're in on something crooked, in other words." Grofield reached out to the bedside table with his good arm, got his Delicados, and lit one. "Now," he said, "it's your turn."

"What kind of cigarette is that?"

"Mexican."

"Well, it smells awful. Put it out. Here." She lifted a corner of her sweater, and a pack of Luckies was tucked into the waistband of her skirt. She tossed it to him, saying, "Light us each one."

He did so, and said, "To repeat, now it's your turn."

"My turn?" She smiled brightly, doing her child routine again. "You mean now I tell you what I know about you?"

"Not yet, Ellen Marie. First you—"

"I wish you wouldn't call me that. My friends call me Elly."

"I'm glad for them. Whenever you go into your act, like Ginger Rogers in *The Major and the Minor*, I'll call you Ellen Marie. Fair enough? Now, tell me your tale of woe."

"I'm not sure I'm going to talk to you at all."

Grofield gestured with his thumb at the door again. "Those three thugs are a lot tougher than any auntie, little girl. You need help to keep clear of them. In fact, you need this room."

"You wouldn't throw me out."

"Not if I know what I'm involved with. But I don't go in blind, that stupid I'm not."

She bit her lip and looked worried. "I suppose you're right," she said at last. "I suppose I've got to let you know the truth."

"It would be a change."

She puffed nervously at the cigarette, and then said, "Did you ever hear of Big Ed Fitzgerald?"

"Big Ed Fitzgerald? No, I can't say I have."

"He tries to keep out of the limelight, avoid publicity, but the papers have written about him a few times. Particularly when he had to go give evidence in front of that Congressional committee."

"Oh? Who is this guy?"

"He's . . . well, he's what they call a kingpin."

"A kingpin."

"In the underworld," she explained, being very earnest now, like a brand-new schoolteacher. "He's very important in organized crime in Philadelphia."

"Oh," said Grofield. "Ah. And this Big Ed Fitzgerald is related to you, is that it?"

"He's my father."

"Your father."

She shook her head and waved both hands, expressing confusion. "I didn't know it myself," she said, "until three years ago, when the committee called him. I just thought he was a building contractor. But he's a lot more than that. He's in the rackets up to his neck."

The last sentence sounded terrible in her mouth, and Grofield winced. "Very graphic," he said.

"Sorry. But he is. He's a kingpin, it said so in the papers."

"The aunties are his boys?"

"Oh, no. They work for someone else, a . . . competitor of my father's. Someone who's trying to—"

"Don't say it. Trying to muscle in?"

She smiled and nodded. "That's right. My father's having a meeting with them in Acapulco on Friday and—"

"You mean like that Apalachin meeting a few years ago."

"But this time they're meeting outside of the country, which is a lot smarter."

"Right."

"Anyway," she said, and gestured vaguely, "anyway, they kidnapped me. They're trying to use me to force my father to go along with what they want. So that's why I've got to stay here until Friday, and then get down to Acapulco to meet him, so he'll know I'm safe."

Grofield motioned at the telephone. "Why not call him now? Why wait till Friday?"

"Because I don't know where he is now. He's incommunicado somewhere, because it would be too dangerous for him right now. These other people might try to kill him."

"So today's— What day is today?"

She seemed surprised. "You don't know what day it is?"

"Honey, when you just lie around in bed forever, one day begins to look pretty much like another."

"Oh. It's Tuesday."

"Tuesday. And you have to be in Acapulco by Friday."

"*On* Friday. I wouldn't dare get there early."

Grofield nodded. "All right," he said, "I think that part's probably the truth. Acapulco on Friday."

"What do you mean, *that* part?"

"Because the rest is pure greasepaint, honey. I remember when Edward Arnold used to play Big Ed Fitzgerald all the time. And didn't Broderick Crawford do it once or twice? Sheldon Leonard was always the heavy, and—"

Abruptly she got up from the bed. "I don't think you ought to make fun of me. I'm all alone, I'm helpless—"

"Oh, come *on!*"

"What about you? I suppose *you* were going to tell *me* the truth!"

Grofield grinned and shook his head. "Not a bit of it. I've got three beauties lined up to tell you, one after the other, each with an all-star cast."

"You just think because you're an inveterate liar everybody else is, too."

"No. Just you."

She opened her mouth to say something else, something angry, but the door opened at the same second and the three hoods came back in, all of them holding guns. The talker smiled in a smug way and said, "Hello there, Miss Fitzgerald. You kind of got lost." He looked at Grofield and made clucking sounds and said, "And you tell lies. We got to do something about that."

4

GROFIELD SAID, "All you people go home. The party doesn't start till five, I don't even have the ashtrays out."

The talker shook his head and said, "You are a very funny man. I wanna keep you with me all the time, to make me laugh when I'm blue. You well enough to walk?"

"A little," Grofield admitted. "Like to the potty and back."

"Like to the elevator and up. Get your clothes on."

One of the others, silent till now, said, "Maybe we just bump him, it's simpler."

The talker looked long-suffering, and shook his head. "And we got the hotel full of cops," he said. "Very bright."

"Maybe he fell out the window. Dizzy from being sick and all."

"You're dizzy. Dead is dead, the hotel is still full of cops. A sick guy, bedridden, what's he doing over by the window?"

Grofield said, "Tell him. I'm on your side."

The talker looked at him. "Then why don't you get dressed?"

The girl said, "Shall I turn my back?"

"Maybe you'd better. Underneath here, I'm horribly scarred."

She made a face and turned around.

Grofield got out of bed slowly, feeling weak but capable of movement. The stiffness that came after sleep had worn off again by now, but he still had no strength. His trousers seemed to weigh a ton, and his fingers were thick and slow-moving and prey to trembles.

The talker said, "You're very slow, pal. You're making me get second thoughts about the window."

"I'm out of practice," Grofield told him. He could feel perspiration beading his face, trickling down his sides, coating his chest and back. The shaking in his fingers had spread up his arms now, and exertion had set waves of dizziness rolling behind his eyes.

The girl said, "Let me help him."

"Fine."

She buttoned his shirt for him, put his shoes on and tied the laces, got his arms into his jacket sleeves, and draped his tie around his neck. "There," she said. "You're beautiful."

"But I've got to leave the ball at midnight, right? Or all this stuff turns back into ermine and silk." He felt lightheaded and foolish, like a drugged prince in a story of palace intrigue in a Carpathian duchy. Background music circled around his head, an unlikely blend of Berg and Debussy. His clothing felt heavy enough to be a prince's uniform, complete with sword buckled at the waist.

"Come on," said the talker. He took Grofield's elbow, not gently.

Grofield deeply regretted his physical condition. He was in trouble now, black trouble, of a source and purpose he didn't understand, and he should be at his most alert and alive for it. Instead, he was woozy and stupid, reeling at the edge of a grave, surrounded by gorillas who might at any time get the notion to shove him on in. Standing, walking, moving his body, he was far more aware of his weakness and vulnerability than when he'd been lying comfortably in bed.

He was being walked now toward the door, and all at once a single thought came pure and clear in his head and he said, "My suitcase." He half-turned toward it, still being tugged the other way by the hand at his elbow.

"You won't need it. You can come back for it."

There it was, halfway across the room, on the rack at the foot of the bed. It was shut, but not locked.

Grofield heard the girl say, "I can carry it for him," and that pleased him, but then the talker said, "I said he don't need it. It stays here to show the chambermaid he hasn't moved out. Saturday, he can come back for it."

"You're a bastard," she said, and even though he was woozy

Grofield understood it was the word *Saturday* that had stung her, and that it had been meant to sting her. So it was true, as he'd supposed, that she had to be somewhere on Friday. Acapulco? Maybe.

The talker was saying now, near Grofield's ear, "You don't need it for nothing, do you? We already got your toothbrush from the bathroom, and you'll be in bed all the time anyway, so what difference does it make?"

Grofield retained sense enough to nod. "It doesn't matter," he said, and they led him out of the room and left the suitcase behind.

PART TWO

1

"I'm sorry," she said.

Grofield said, "Sorry? What for? What's to be sorry about?"

"You're mad at me," she said.

Grofield said, "Give me another cigarette." He'd left his Delicados downstairs.

They were in the room directly above his old one. The hoods had rented a suite up here, three rooms with this one in the middle. There was a hall door, but it was double-locked and the key was gone, so you could only get in and out through the rooms on either side.

And the window, of course. You could still go out the window, except the hoods had stripped the bedding from the bed, removed the curtains from the window, and even taken away Grofield's belt. There was nothing to use as a rope anymore, so there wouldn't be any more trips out the window.

Grofield and Ellen Marie Fitzgerald were alone now, Grofield half-sitting and half-lying on the bare mattress, the girl prowling the room in nervous agitation. They'd been brought here five minutes ago and left alone, and until now neither of them had done any talking. The way Grofield felt, the silence could have gone on forever.

But the girl had things to say, nice, useful things like *I'm sorry*. She also wanted to make amends; when Grofield asked her for a cigarette, she lit it herself before handing it to him. There was a faint trace of lipstick on the tip. She stood beside the bed, lit a second cigarette for herself, and said, "I'm sorry about the—"

Grofield quickly overrode her, saying, "The way I see it, the only reason your pals left us alone like this is to hear what we have to say."

Her eyes widened, and she glanced toward one of the side doors. "You think so? Why?"

"To see where I fit in, see if we know each other from somewhere. You ready to tell me the truth now?"

She hesitated, biting her lower lip. Finally she said, "No, I can't. I wish I could, I owe you at least that much, but—"

"You owe me plenty, honey."

"I know. Believe me, I know, and I can't tell you how sorry I am."

"You can't tell me much of anything, can you?"

"No. I just can't, that's all."

Grofield said, "But there is a place you have to be by Friday. Or *on* Friday."

"Yes. On Friday, yes."

"And it's the place you said before."

"Acapulco, yes." She saw him glance at the door, and said, "Oh, they know about it. That's why they're holding me. They'll let us both go on Saturday, I know they will."

Grofield said, "I'm not sure I can wait."

"I *know* I can't wait. But what can I do?" And, looking wild-eyed, she went back to the pacing again.

Grofield let the silence stretch between them again, for several reasons. In the first place, he expected any minute she'd make a slip and say something about the money. In the second place, he wanted time to think about where he was and work out a way to be somewhere else.

He hated the weakness of his body now, its stiffness and sluggishness. He was never sick, always in good physical shape, his actor's preparations having included fencing lessons and tumbling, some acrobatics and horsemanship and ballroom dancing, so that he was ready at any time to take a role in *The Prisoner of Zenda*. Any time but now, when he needed it.

Plus, as if the wound weren't handicap enough, he was completely off his home field. He'd never been in Mexico before, had no tourist papers, didn't speak the language. Except for the clothes he had on—and the suitcase full of money—he had no luggage, nothing to wear, nothing. He was unarmed, he had no local contacts or friends, and he didn't dare go to either the Mexican police or the American Embassy.

The more he thought about it, the more he had to accept the fact that he needed this girl's help. She'd gotten him into a mess he couldn't handle as a single, and she could damn well cooperate to get him out again.

She was still pacing over there, looking panicky but intent. He said, "Come here."

She stopped, startled for a second, and then reoriented herself and came over toward him, but not close enough. He gestured impatiently for her to sit down on the bed next to him. She got a mistrustful look on her face, but he let her know with his own look of disgust that she'd guessed wrong. She said, "What—?" but he cut her off with a violent arm gesture that obviously meant *shut up*.

When she finally sat down, elbow to elbow with him, their legs stretched out parallel in front of them on the bare mattress, he whispered, "This is the way we have a private conversation. Get it?"

"I'm sorry," she whispered back. "I didn't catch on fast enough, I was thinking about other things."

"You're sorry a lot, aren't you? All right, never mind, just listen. There are things each of us wants."

She nodded vigorously.

"So we help each other," he whispered. "You help me get out of here and get my suitcase back. I help you get to Acapulco on Friday."

"It's a deal," she said, maybe too quickly.

Grofield looked at her, and she was as sweet and innocent as a ten-year-old nun. Unicorn bait. And in the brain behind those eyes, Grofield was convinced, she was planning to ditch him, with or without the money, the first chance she got.

Well, the hell. You had to work with the materials at hand. Grofield whispered, "What about papers? You in the country legally?"

33

"Of course." She seemed honestly surprised, so surprised she almost answered aloud.

"Ssst! Keep it down."

"Sorry. I—"

"Again? Sorry again?"

"I do say that all the time, don't I?"

"You have cause. What about a driver's license? Got one?"

"Yes."

"On you?"

"In my bra. I put all my papers there when I went out the window."

"Fine. And here comes the capper. This is the one you've got to answer straight."

"If I can."

"You can. When you climbed down that sheet, the phone to call the cops is not where you headed. If we get away again, will your aunties call the cops?"

"Are you kidding?"

"Our deal is still on either way," Grofield assured her. "It's just we'll have to work things different on the outside."

She sat up straighter, half-turned to face him, held up her right hand in the three-fingered Scout pledge. "I guarantee," she whispered fiercely, "those rotten bastards have never spoken willingly to the police in their entire lives and nothing about what's going on now is going to change that. They will not call the police, I swear it."

"All right. Good. So the next thing is to get out of here."

"You make it sound easy."

"Don't you believe me. Help me off this bed."

"All right."

She scrambled off first, took his right arm, and helped him through that no-man's-land of balance between sitting down and standing up. Once he was vertical he was all right.

He looked around the room, and it was discouragingly bare. With the curtains off the window and the covers off the bed, the place looked naked, vacant, nobody home.

Aside from the bed, there was the normal minimum of hotel-room furniture; a metal dresser with a fake wood veneer, a floor lamp with an atrocious pink shade, a Danish-modern armchair with green leatherette seat and back, a small writing table and chair in a style to match the dresser, and a low luggage rack at the foot of the bed.

Grofield said, "Don't you have any gear? Luggage?"

"In the closet."

"Get it out, let's see if there's anything we can use."

From the closet she got two small white suitcases, very expensive looking. She set them both on the bed, opened them, and stepped back. "Take a look," she said. "No guns or knives or hand grenades."

"Oh, shucks," said Grofield. "I had such high hopes." He went over and, right-handed, poked through both suitcases.

It was all normal goods. Cashmere sweaters, cotton blouses, wool skirts. Bras and panties and stockings and garter belts, but no girdle. Four pairs of shoes, of varying styles, and some rolled pairs of socks. Toothbrush and toothpaste and a whole array of toilet articles and cosmetics.

She said, *sotto voce*, as he kept poking, "You know, I'm beginning to get scared."

"That's all right," he said, distracted, thinking about other things. What to use, how to use it, what's the plan.

"Running away from them," she went on, her whisper turning shrill, "sneaking away, that was one thing. But you mean to *attack* them, have us fight our way through them."

"Only way. We might tie bits of clothing together, make another rope, but I wouldn't trust it to hold."

"No."

"Nor me to hold onto it. My left arm isn't much use. I can hold a cup or a spoon with it, but that's about all."

"So we have to go through them."

"Center of the line," he said. "Off tackle."

"But there are three of them, and they're all healthy, and they're armed. And there are two of us, and we are half unhealthy and half a girl, and we aren't armed."

"Yes, yes."

"Maybe we should wait and see what—"

He held up a can, saying, "What's this stuff?"

"What? Oh, hair spray. You know, to hold a set."

"This is one of these pressure cans, right? And the stuff sprays out the top here." He gave an experimental push to the button on top, and a brief fog hissed out. "Doesn't go far," he commented. "Dissipates in a hurry. You ever get this stuff in your eyes?"

"Lord, no. It stings like fury."

"How do you know?"

"Well, I got a little in my eye once. It stings like soap, only worse. They tell you on the can, be sure and keep it out of your eyes."

"Fine." He went over and set the can on the dresser. "Weapon number one," he said, and went back to the suitcases.

She said, "Hair spray? Against guns?"

"You packed this thing, I didn't."

"We'd better wait, really and truly. Maybe we'll get a chance to sneak away again, and—"

He turned and said, "In the first place, no. In the second place, they'll be watching you closer this time and you won't be getting any more chances to sneak away. In the third place, I can't afford to wait. In the fourth place, we can't just take off, we've got to lock *them* up before we do, so we'll have a head start on them and I can stop off for my suitcase. And in the fifth place, don't talk so loud, they might still be listening."

"Oh. Sorry."

"And in the sixth place, stop saying sorry." He went back to the suitcases again, and came up with a small pair of scissors in a clear plastic case. "What's this?"

"Nail scissors."

"Nail scissors. A weapon?"

"They have blunt tips. Rounded tips."

"Too bad." He tossed them on the bed. "We'll think about them some more later. What else, now?"

But there didn't seem to be anything else. Reluctantly, Grofield gave up on the suitcases and looked around the room again, but the room itself was still as bare as ever. He went into the bathroom, a small white place with a vent instead of a window, and found nothing there either.

Back in the main room, he said, "All right, we work with what we've got."

"But we don't have anything," she said.

"Sshh, quiet."

Grofield prowled around the room, looking at this and that, thinking. He listened at the doors on both sides, hearing radio music from the room on the left and low conversation from the room on the right. So that was the disposition of forces, two and one.

She said, "They don't want to kill us, but they will if they have to."

"That's the way I feel, too," Grofield said. He unplugged the lamp, took the nail scissors, and cut the electric cord near the base of the lamp. He stripped about an inch of the two wires bare at the cut end, fastened these to the metal knob and lock of the door through which he'd heard the radio playing, and plugged the other end in again.

She said, "Won't that kill somebody?"

"I don't know. Maybe. Maybe it'll just knock him out. He won't be coming in here, I'll tell you that much."

"I think you scare me," she said.

Grofield flashed her his winning smile. "It's only nature," he told her. "The lioness defending her cub, the patriot defending his nation, me getting back to my suitcase. You don't know the months of worry-free art that suitcase is going to provide me."

"Art? Are you a painter?"

"There's art and art," Grofield said. He was disappointed in her. But then he smiled again and patted her cheek. "Don't you worry your pretty head, Missy. We'll see the plantation again."

"But it will never be the same," she said. "Never."

Grofield liked her again now. He laughed and said, "Onward. Step two."

Among the toilet articles in her luggage was a fresh cake of sweet-smelling soap. He took this, and a white sock, and went into the bathroom, where he filled the sink with steaming water, too hot to touch. He put the soap in the sock, then draped the sock over the edge of the sink so the soap was submerged.

She watched him uncomprehending, and finally said, "What's all that about?"

"Product of a misspent youth," he told her. "We'll let it sit five minutes or so, and then we'll see."

"Some day," she said, "you're going to have to tell me all about yourself."

He laughed. "Right after you tell me all about you," he said. He went back to the living room and looked out the window; it was raining. "Must be four o'clock."

Behind him, she looked at her watch and said, "Five after. How did you know?"

He pointed a thumb at the window. "Rain. It always rains at four o'clock here in the summer."

"Is that right? I just got here this morning, I—that can't be right. Every day?"

"Almost. It'll be over in five or ten minutes, and the sun'll come back out." He looked around the room. With the clouds and the rain, the room was somewhat dim, even though the window was bare. "We better make our move before then," he said.

"What are we going to do?"

"An oldie. I'm going to have a sudden relapse, groaning and carrying on, on the bed. You hammer on the door—that one, not the one I wired—and call for help. They—"

"They won't believe it," she said. "Even *I* wouldn't believe it. They did that in every western movie ever made."

"I know. But I am sick and they know it, so it's more likely to be legit in their eyes. Besides, I'll holler my head off, and they'll be in a hurry to stop me."

"All right," she said. "It's worth a try. So they come in. Now what?"

"One or two of them come in," he said. "In any case, we can figure only one of them will come over to me. The other will stay in the doorway, probably, or just a step or two inside the room. Now, the one who comes over to the bed is mine." He picked up the can of hair spray and said, "I'll use this on him, as soon as he gets close enough."

"What if he doesn't get close enough?"

"He will. The way I'll be hollering, he'll get close enough."

"All right. What do I do?"

"You take care of number two."

"Good of me," she said.

"Clever of you, in fact. Come here, let's see if it's ready."

They went back to the bathroom and Grofield took the sock out of the water. "It'll do," he said, studying it critically. "Give me a towel, we'll dry this."

She handed him a towel, and said, "I still don't get it. Am I stupid?"

"No. Merely overprotected." He folded the sock in the towel, patted it dry, put the towel down, and walked back into the bedroom. "What we have here," he told her, "is a homemade blackjack."

"We do?"

"Right. The hot water melted the outer edge of the soap a little, and now as it hardens again, the sock sticks to it and you've got a nice, hard handy cosh here." He held the sock by the loose upper end and showed it to her. "The other way," he said, "is to fill the sock with sand, but we don't have any sand."

"Does it really work?"

"Guaranteed. Just swing it with all your might. If his back is to you, which we dearly hope it is, go for the head. If he's facing you, go for the stomach, swing sidearm. Then, when he bends over, give him the second one in the head."

"I'm not sure I—"

"Acapulco?"

"I know," she said. "But I've never done anything like this before."

"There's nothing to it," he told her. "Just keep your hands by your side when they first come in, so your skirt hides the sap. Wait till I make my move, and then you go for number two."

"But what if I don't do it right?"

"Don't worry about it. If you keep swinging, you can't go wrong. Besides, I should have the other one's gun pretty quick. At the very worst, you'll be distracting him while I take care of his buddy."

She shook her head. "I don't know," she said. "It was a lot easier to just go out the window."

"Five flights up? If that didn't scare you, this won't."

"It scared me, believe me it did."

"And you did it anyway. So you'll do this anyway." He lay

39

down on the bed, the spray can in his right hand tucked down against his right hip. The door was to his left, so the can should be out of sight until he was ready to use it. He looked over at her standing by the door and said, "You ready?"

She gave him a weak smile, a shrug, and a nod.

"Okay. Let me groan a few seconds first, build it up, before you start on the door."

She nodded again.

Grofield closed his eyes and got into character.

Now and again his two occupations complemented each other. Grofield the professional thief had worked out the escape plan from this room, but it was Grofield the professional actor who put the plan into operation.

Who was he? Where was he? The underfurnished room, the bare mattress, the curtainless window, the girl standing apprehensive by the closed door . . . it was France, 1942. Outside, the German soldiers have just driven up in two trucks, following the jeep full of Gestapo men. Here, inside the farmhouse, lies the wounded British aviator, being hidden and cared for by the farm family with the beautiful daughter. Everything at this moment hinges on his silence, but he is unconscious, delirious, feverish, terribly wounded . . .

He thrashed a little bit on the bed. Eyes squeezed shut, he began to moan.

$\mathcal{2}$

"HELP! HELP!"

She was doing beautifully, hollering away and hammering her fists on the door. On the bed, Grofield was screaming like a banshee and waving his right arm in the air.

The door burst open so fast that Ellen Marie barely had time to jump back out of the way and get the cosh down out of sight. Grofield, doing it right, let another notch out of his voice and projected a howl straight through the ceiling.

Both of them had come charging into the room, guns drawn. It was the talker and one of his assistants. The talker yelled at everybody at once, trying to be heard over Grofield's shrieking, "Shut up! What is it? Watch her! Shut your face, you!"

He came running toward the bed. The other one, open-mouthed, stood in the middle of the room and paid no attention to Ellen Marie, but gaped at Grofield instead. Grofield's waving arm dropped down to his side, fingers folding around the spray can.

But the talker had his own methods. He didn't want to know what Grofield's problem was, he just wanted to shut Grofield's mouth. So he came running to the bed, reversing the gun in his hand, and immediately swung the gun butt in a long, rapid loop aimed straight at Grofield's head.

Grofield, his eyes half-closed, saw it coming just barely in time and wrenched himself out of the way with a jolting effort that drew the kind of knife pain from his wound that he hadn't felt in two days. The gun butt smashed into the mattress next to Grofield's ear.

He'd lost the can. It was down there somewhere, he almost had it, but his finger couldn't find the button on top. He just grabbed it, swung with it.

The talker had wound up his swing half-bent over the bed, enraged face directly above Grofield's. Before he could regain his balance, Grofield had swung around and hit him in the mouth with the side of the spray can.

But the can was too light. It startled the talker, but that's all it did. Grofield hit him two more times fast with the can, once again on the mouth and once on the nose, and only dented the can. But by then he'd finally found the button, and he started spraying.

Only he was too late. The talker was already backing away from the bed, getting control of things again, reversing the gun to get the long-distance end aimed at Grofield. Grofield had managed to cut his lip, but that wasn't enough, not nearly enough.

Nor could he get off the bed in time. The useless spray can still clutched in his hand, Grofield struggled around on the bed, trying to get up, trying to get on his feet. His left arm didn't want to help at all, didn't want to do a thing.

In front of him, too far away, the talker had come to a stop, was braced, had the gun around and aimed, was saying, "Goodbye, you smart bas—"

And fell over on his face.

Grofield had managed finally to get off the bed by throwing himself over the edge. He and the talker hit the floor at the same time. The talker's gun bounced and landed beside Grofield's cheek. Grofield looked up and saw Ellen Marie standing there, the only vertical person in the room.

She shook her head and hefted the blackjack. "I don't know what you'd do without me," she said.

"You got him?"

"I got them both."

"Bless you, Elly. You're a dear child."

"There's a rumor going around," she said, "that *you're* going to help *me*."

"Moral support," he said. "Also, I hold your coat. Would you mind helping me up? I believe I've had enough humiliation for one day."

She helped him to his feet and handed him the talker's gun, then pointed at the other door. "I haven't heard a thing from there," she said. "Shouldn't we have heard something?"

"What?"

"I don't know. A scream maybe."

"Or sizzling?"

"Oh! Don't talk like that."

"Wait here," he said. "I'll go around and see."

She said, "What if these two start to wake up again?"

"Conk them again."

"Is that safe?"

"Sure. It's soft, won't cut the flesh or anything."

"But what about concussions?"

"I don't know," he admitted. "What about them? Wait here, I'll be right back."

"All right."

He went through the other room, out to the hall, down past the locked door to the room where he'd been imprisoned, and tried the door to room number three. It was unlocked, and inside, hood number three was lying on his face on the floor.

Grofield went over and looked at him and he looked very gray. Grofield called through the door, "Unplug that thing."

"All right. Wait a second."

Grofield waited till she told him it was all right, then unlocked and opened the door. "There," he said. "Our choice of escape routes."

She looked past him, saying, "Is he—is he—?"

"I don't know. Does it matter?"

"Yes, it does. I've never, I've never been involved in—would you please go see how he is?"

"If you say so." Grofield went over and knelt beside him and looked him over. "He's breathing," he said. "Shallow, but breath."

"I'm glad."

He looked up at her, and she really did mean it. She wasn't, so far as he could tell, totally consistent. One minute she was climbing up and down the outside of buildings on a sheet and knocking out gunmen with a homemade cosh, and the next minute she was Louisa May Alcott.

Skipping right out of Alcott again, now, she said briskly, "Shouldn't we hurry? We've still got to get away from here."

"One thing at a time, sweetheart. Help me drag this guy into the other room."

He was feeling very down now, after the sudden burst of activity. Also, his throat was sore from all the shrieking he'd done. Dragging the limp body into the middle room, even with Ellen Marie's help, left him shaking with weakness. He sat down on the bed, gasping a little, saying, "Got to rest a minute. Look, you go through that side room, lock the door behind you, take the key with you, come around through the hall and come back here, okay?"

"You all right?"

"I'm fine. I just have to sit down a minute, that's all."

"Your face is all-over sweat. Let me get you a towel."

"You're a dear girl."

She got him the towel and then went away to lock the connecting door. Grofield mopped his face and looked at the three sleeping beauties. "I would like to see you boys again some time," he told them, "when I'm up to snuff."

Ellen Marie came back in from the hall and said, "Now what?"

"Get their guns and their wallets and any official-type papers they may have on them, and pack everything away in your suitcase. Then we're getting out of here."

"Good. Where do we go from here?"

"First, down to get my suitcase. Second, out of the hotel and into a cab. Third, to a car-rental agency, where you are going to rent a car. Fourth, out of Mexico City."

"I can't go to Acapulco," she said. "I don't dare get there before Friday. There are more of—" she motioned at the three on the floor "—more of them down there. That's why I came here; I thought I'd be safe here until Friday."

"But they were waiting for you."

"Yes."

"So we'll go somewhere else." He felt more rested now, and much more pleased with life. He got to his feet, staggering almost not at all, and said, "A place I've heard of. We'll both love it. Come on."

They locked the hoods in, and went away.

3

THE CAR WAS a Datsun, a Japanese make, cream-colored, with automatic gearshift. A two-door sedan, it was a little cramped for Grofield's long legs, but not bad. It was a family-type pleasure-type car, sturdy and reliable, but not very peppy. Grofield, at the wheel, had the feeling he'd have trouble getting away from even a determined cyclist.

Still, it was a pleasant little car, about the size of an American compact. Their luggage was on the back seat, two suitcases each now, Grofield having taken extra time to do some shopping for clothes and a bag to put them in.

Late afternoon in Mexico City. Always a good time of day, after the rain, with the sun out again and a bright, fresh, newly washed look to the world. Grofield drove west along Paseo de la Reforma, one of the two major thoroughfares of the city and its more beautiful. Eight lanes of two-way traffic were flanked by broad swaths of green grass. Statues, benches, and pedestrian paths lined these strips of grass, beyond which were narrow access streets paralleling the main lanes, and then finally the buildings. Movie houses, banks, hotels, and government buildings flanked Reforma. The Mexico City Hilton was here, and the American Embassy. At each major intersection there was a circle around a large monument; the statue of Charles IV, the statue of Columbus, the statue of Cuauhtémoc, and finally the Independence Monument, a great golden-winged figure called "the Angel."

Farther west, Reforma turned at an angle to the right and cut through Chapultepec Park. Great trees arched over the roadway, roofing it in green, so that they drove through a dappled effect of light and shadow, the park stretching away on both sides. The *peseros*, one-peso taxicabs of red or yellow or dark green, raced by in both directions, the traffic crowded but surprisingly fast.

Ellen Marie lit two cigarettes, gave Grofield one, and said, "This is a beautiful city. I think I'd like to come here sometime."

"You mean when you can look at it."

"Something like that."

Grofield glanced at her, sitting easy and relaxed beside him. Light and shadow, light and shadow; sunlight did very good things for her hair. "I can't figure out what sort of mess you could get yourself in," he said.

"Don't try. Please."

Grofield shrugged. "Patience is my middle name," he said.

"Is Alan really your first?"

"Yes."

"Thank, thank you, Alan, for helping me."

"Sure. What did I do?"

"You made the blackjack."

Grofield grinned. "Any time," he said.

At the end of Chapultepec Park, at a huge statue-fountain affair that looked like the world's biggest bookend, Grofield turned right off Reforma and onto Avenue Manuel Avila Comacho. He'd spent five minutes looking at a road map in the car-rental office, and now he was a little surprised it was all going as easily as the map had made it look.

She said, "You haven't told me yet where we're going. Is it a surprise?"

"For both of us. I've never been there myself, but I've heard of it. It's north of here about—"

"North? But Acapulco is south. Shouldn't we at least go *toward* Acapulco and stop off somewhere along the way until Friday?"

"No, not a bit of it. I looked at the map, and as far as I can see, there's only the one road to Acapulco. It goes through Taxco, and then on down to the coast. It's the only road to Acapulco from anywhere, so all your friends have to do is start at one end and search for us until they find us."

"Oh. I didn't realize that. Only the one road?"

"Only the one road."

"But that's ridiculous. Acapulco is a big city, a resort city."

"One road."

"Good Lord, no place has only one road. I mean, there's always at least a north-south road and an east-west road, and that's two. And actually four, because you can come from each direction."

"Not Acapulco. According to the map, there's the road from Mexico City and that's all. It comes from the north into Acapulco and stops. South of Acapulco is the ocean. East and west is the coastline, but there's no road along it. Maybe there will be some day, but there isn't now."

"Then how are we going to get there?"

"We'll worry about that," he told her, "when the time comes. What we're going to do now is go north, to a place called San Miguel de Allende. We'll stay there until—When do you have to be in Acapulco? What time Friday?"

"Just before midnight, that's all."

"All right. Friday morning, early, we'll leave San Miguel and head for Acapulco and see what happens."

"But if there's only the one road—"

"We'll see what happens."

"All right," she said. "We'll see what happens."

4

ELLY CLIMBED OUT of the pool, tweaked flesh in at the bottom of her bathing suit, brushed wet hair back from her face with her palms, and came walking toward Grofield.

Grofield, in a bathing suit, sitting on the grass in the sunlight and holding a bottle of Carta Blanca beer in his hand, was well pleased with life. The late-morning sun was warm, the air was clear, the surroundings were pleasant, his wound felt fine, and the girl walking toward him looked incredible in a pale blue two-piece bathing suit. He smiled lazily, gestured with the beer bottle, looked up at Elly through a new pair of sunglasses, and said, "Howdy, comrade. Set a spell."

"Comrade," she agreed. She flopped down on the ground beside him, took the beer away from him, swallowed a healthy portion, and gave it back. "You ought to go in the water," she said.

"My bandage."

"We've got to change it anyway. Besides, it's spring water, it's warm, it'll be great for your wound."

"The sun is great enough. I'm content."

She looked around and nodded judiciously. "You've redeemed yourself," she said.

"Honey, I told you last night I'd never been to San Miguel before. I'd heard about it, friends of mine told me about it. They said it's the Greenwich Village of Mexico, it's full of American painters and writers and composers and whatnot, all on six-month tourist permits, because it's supposed to be cheap and great—"

"And ugly," she finished.

"No. And beautiful. I was talking to the barman; he says San Miguel is a national monument. They've got two, this one and Taxco, both national monuments. You can't build anything or tear anything down without permission from the federal government."

"Is that why they don't fix the streets?"

"Cobblestones. It's Old Mexico, preserved for the modern day. I thought it looked great, myself."

She nodded. "Me too. I'm glad we went through it, it was very nice. I'd love to look at it forever, but I wouldn't want to *live* there for a minute. That hotel was just a little too Old Mexico for me. I'm New America myself." She stretched, which looked fine. "One thing, at least," she said. "Honner won't ever think to look for us there."

"Honner?"

"The man you sprayed."

"Honner."

She stretched again. "Well, what do we do now?"

"We wait. We can go back into town tonight, see what the night life is like."

"I can imagine what the night life is like. But all right, we'll go."

"I won't twist your arm."

"Will you come in the water?"

"Maybe later on."

"I'm going now, I don't want to get a burn."

"See you."

She got to her feet and stretched some more. Over at the other pool, the round one with the hot water in it, a couple of the old men sitting at the rim kept looking at Elly and shaking their heads, looking at her and scratching their stomachs, looking at her and kicking their feet a little in the water. Grofield watched them watch her go to the warm-water pool and dive in. Then they looked away, started talking real estate together again, and Grofield took another swig of beer.

This was a good place, about six miles north of town, in on its own dirt road from the blacktop road between San Miguel and a town called Dolores Hidalgo. The hotel was called the Taboada

Balneario, and it was all by itself in the semi-arid plain. The buildings were long and low, in a combination of Indian and Spanish styles, with red tile roofs; thick-trunked trees were intermixed with the buildings. There were the two spring-fed swimming pools, one containing hot and the other warm water, plus a large dining room with one long window-wall facing the main lawn and pools. A bus came up from San Miguel once a day, bringing tourists to take pictures and swim in the pool, but they hadn't arrived yet, and at the moment the place was nearly empty.

They'd found it almost by accident. Coming into town about seven-thirty last night, they'd both been unprepared for just how primitive a national monument could be. They'd looked at two hotels, one of which had a great central courtyard, but neither of which Elly would agree to stay in, and then Grofield saw a lavender Lincoln slowly poking its way along the narrow street, like a panther in a maze. The Lincoln had California plates, so Grofield stopped it, asked the driver to recommend a place, and the driver—an arrogant-looking fat man of about fifty—looked Grofield over, said, "middle income," as though to himself, and then told them about the Taboada Balneario.

Nervous reaction from the excitement of the day had set in with Elly, who by then was being irritable and jumpy. She wouldn't make sense when Grofield asked her if she thought they ought to make the extra drive and see what this place looked like, so he just drove it and the hell with her. He'd taken adjoining rooms without looking at them, he'd stuffed Elly and her luggage into one of them without letting her talk to him word one, and he'd gone into his own room and to bed and to sleep, promptly.

And this morning everything was fine. They were both rested and feeling easy, and the hotel was great, although hotel was maybe not exactly the word for it. The rooms were more or less motel fashion, in a row, with separate entrances, but Grofield had never seen a motel before with a brick ceiling. An honest-to-God brick ceiling; he'd spent about an hour this morning lying in bed and looking up at it, wondering why it didn't fall down. It looked like a brick wall up there, but it was horizontal.

The hotel was on the American plan, meals included. They had a slow and leisurely breakfast together, then walked around the grounds a while before changing into bathing suits.

Grofield continued to sit there after Elly went back into the pool. He drank his beer, felt the sun warm on his back, and began to feel more and more like his old self.

Later on he did go in the pool for a while, and the warm water was fine for the wound, but not so good for the bandage, which was getting old anyway, having been put on five days ago. After the bus came from San Miguel, bringing tourists with cameras and natives in wool bathing suits, they went back to their rooms and she got the gauze and tape she'd bought yesterday to change his bandage.

He lay on his stomach on his bed while she sat beside him and cut the old bandage off. The water had loosened it from the wound, so it came off readily enough, and she said, "That's ugly."

"Thank you."

"I've never seen a bullet wound before. Do they all look like that?"

"No. Some of them have a lot of green pus coming out."

"Ugh. Wait there a minute." She left the bed, threw the old bandage away, went over to the bathroom and came back a minute later with a wet cloth. "Let me know if this hurts," she said, and started swabbing the wound.

"Uh," he said. "It doesn't feel funny."

"All done." Putting a fresh bandage on, she said, "Is the bullet still in there?"

"No. A doctor took it out. The one who put the bandage on."

"I suppose you were shot while you were stealing all that money."

"Tell me about Acapulco," he said.

"All right, never mind. I won't pry."

"You're a nice girl."

"All done," she said, and stood up. "I put a smaller one on this time. It looks almost healed."

"Don't let it fool you," he said, rolling over. "You can't tell a wound from its scab."

54

"What a charming way you have with the language."

She was standing beside the bed, a sexy Florence Nightingale in her bathing suit and her hands full of gauze and tape. He grinned up at her, feeling the old urge, and reached up to touch one finger to the bone of her left wrist. Slowly he moved that finger up her forearm to her elbow, then closed his hand around her arm, tugging her gently closer. She didn't resist, and her smile as she looked down at him was faintly quizzical.

Still smiling at her, he said, "One thing I want you to know."

"What's that?"

"I'm married."

She burst out laughing. "Oh, my God!"

This was the first girl he'd turned his attentions toward since tying the knot. If they were all going to react to the news that way, it was going to be hell. And yet, not to tell them would be to leave himself open to a vast array of unthinkable complications.

Done laughing, she looked at him and shook her head and said, "That is the God damnedest line-opener I've heard in my life, and believe me, I've heard some dandies."

"I believe you."

"Are you really married? Or is that just a thing you say so the girl won't try to make a thing of it?"

"Both."

"Is your wife nice?"

"She was the last time I saw her. God knows what she's like now. But I doubt that she'd mind if I kissed you."

"Nonsense."

"You think she'd mind?" Grofield asked, putting on an innocent face at least as good as the one Elly sometimes used.

"Yes, I do," she said, in mock seriousness.

"Then let's not tell her."

Elly smiled. "All right," she said. "Let's not."

Grofield tugged at her arm again. She slid toward him.

5

ELLY SAID, "This is the night life, huh?"

"What's the matter?" Grofield asked her. "Aren't you thrilled, baby? *I'm* thrilled."

They were back in San Miguel again, in a bar on the main square, where they'd been told they could find the center of the town's night life. The bar was called La Cucaracha; a brown real-as-life figure of a cockroach, about a foot and a half long, was mounted at an angle on one wall.

The room itself was simply a small square full of seats, with a jukebox jutting out on one side. There was no bar, there were no more signs inside than there'd been outside—they'd had a hell of a time finding the place, since from the street it didn't look as though there was anything here at all—and generally speaking, it was hard to convince yourself you were in a bar. Since the chairs and sofas were all done in plastic and foam rubber, the place looked most of all like the world's most crowded doctor's waiting room.

Every once in a while, Sancho Panza in a dirty apron would come through and take orders and go away again, coming back a while later with either what you asked for or something else.

The people here reminded Grofield of home, but that was because he'd lived at one time in Greenwich Village. Along Mac-dougal and Eighth streets the same faces could be found in all the tourist traps: the tourists themselves, looking embarrassed and irritable, and the unwashed, unshaven youngsters living around here while going through their artistic phase, looking both older and younger than their years. Both the tourists and the young-sters were self-conscious, and neither could cover it all the way.

But here there was a third kind of person, too. Around San Miguel there was a colony of retired people from the States, living on pensions. A thousand dollars a year was damn good money on the local economy, so these retired people could live in a climate as good as Florida or California, but at a fraction of the price. Their presence somehow made both the tourists and the youngsters look even more foolish than usual, as though some-how or other they'd been exposed as frauds.

It was now about nine o'clock at night. Grofield and Elly had come into town after dinner, had window-shopped in some of the local stores—silver and straw were the main materials used in the goods for sale—had wandered around looking at the old houses and the old streets that made this a national monument, and now had come in here to see what was doing.

Elly said, "If we hurry back to the hotel, we can go moonlight swimming in the pool."

"What's the matter? The pace here too much for you?"

"Something like that."

"Okay. Drink up."

They finished their drinks and sidestepped among knees to the door. Outside, the air was clear and the night dark. In front of them was a plaza or square, all complicated flowers and greenery, with geometric paths and ornamental fences, and with a band-stand in the middle. A single light bulb gleamed in the middle of the bandstand ceiling.

She said, "Let's take a walk over there. By the bandstand."

"Kay."

They walked across the cobbled street and through the little park, hand in hand, and up onto the bandstand. Under the light, Grofield kissed her. She was warm and slender and soft, her blouse electric beneath his hand.

They went down off the bandstand on the other side and walked around the square, which was flanked on three sides by small shops and bars and eateries, all with either the most modest of signs or no signs at all, and on the fourth side by a large pretentious Gothic church. They walked around on the strip of sidewalk bordering the park, and all at once she stopped, squeezing his hand. "Don't move!"

It was whispered, but it was shrill and urgent. Grofield stopped and didn't move. He looked around and saw nothing, no one walking, no one in sight. There was the church, with some cars parked in front of it, and the shops with cars parked in front, and that was it.

"In front of the church," she whispered.

He whispered back, "What? What is it?"

"The Pontiac. The green Pontiac with the whitewalls. It's their car."

"Honner?"

"Yes." Her arm was trembling against his. "Honner," she said.

THERE WAS not much light. The only really bright illumination came from the bulb in the ceiling of the bandstand. Windows and doorways here and there around the square spread dim amber rectangles of light on the cobblestones, and from the doorway of La Cucaracha came the dim sound of the jukebox, playing Mexican guitar music.

A group of youngsters, chattering in Spanish, came up the hill on the other side of the square, turned left at the corner, walked away, out of sight and out of hearing.

Grofield whispered, "Sit down on the bench here. Don't move. Don't make any noise."

"Where are you going?"

"Just be quiet."

He moved away from her, into the park, skirting the edge of the park just outside the ring of light from the bandstand. When he was on the side opposite the church and the Pontiac, he stopped to watch and listen.

No one. Nothing moved.

He crossed the street, moving with silent, loping speed, turned right on the narrow sidewalk in front of the shops, moved back around the square again to the church, this time keeping close against the buildings.

Two couples left La Cucaracha, talking loudly together in English, their voices sounding hollow on the silent air, as though they were in an armory or an airplane hangar. They moved away, down a side street.

An automobile nosed its way into the square, drove around three sides, and finally came to a stop at a place reserved for taxis. The headlights went off, the driver got out and locked the car, and went away. He wore a cap, he had a black moustache, and his white shirt was bunched like a life preserver around his waist. As he walked away, he rubbed the back of his hand across his mouth as though he were thirsty.

Grofield moved down the row of cars in a half-crouch, came to the Pontiac, stopped beside it. It was empty and the doors were locked.

He moved around to the front and opened the hood. It made a loud sound that rang in the silence, like the sound an oven makes when it's cooling. Grofield reached in, unable to see what he was doing, and ripped every wire he could get his hands on. When he was finished, he left the hood open; it would make too much noise to shut it.

He went straight across the street now to where he'd left Elly. She was sitting on the bench where he'd told her to wait. He whispered, "Phase one. They aren't there. Wait here some more."

"Where are you going now?"

He squatted down on his heels and rubbed his palms and fingers on the grass, wiping the grease from the Pontiac off them. "The only way they could have found us," he said, "is through the car-rental office. They must have checked them out this morning, with lots of pesos and a good story, and the clerk we talked to yesterday told them all about us, and how I studied the road maps for San Miguel de Allende."

"They're fast, Alan," she whispered. "That's why they scare me, they're so fast. And Honner's a lot smarter than he looks."

"We'll see. The point is, they're sure to have a description of the car. I figure that's where I'll find them."

"You're going after them?"

"I've got to. We can't get back to the hotel without the car. And our luggage is back there, remember? Luggage."

"Oh," she said. "The suitcase."

"I'm beginning to regret that suitcase," he said. "I admit it freely. Money is a burden. I may write a monograph on the subject." He stood up. "Later on. I'll be back soon. You be ready to jump aboard."

"All right."

He moved away, taking one of the captured guns from his hip pocket. He'd brought it along as an extra precaution, feeling a little foolish to be carrying it but preferring to feel foolish rather than naked. This was the smallest of the three guns they'd taken away from Honner and his friends, a .25-caliber automatic from Italy, the Beretta Jetfire. Little more than a toy with its tiny grip and two-inch barrel, it would do the job at the kind of range Grofield might want it for.

Carrying it in his right hand, he moved off again into the darkness at the edges of the square. He was still moving cautiously, but more quickly than before, sure he'd find all three of them near the car.

The car was three blocks away, downhill. The street to it was lit at long intervals by light standards containing low-watt bulbs. It was a narrow street, cobblestoned, uneven, hemmed in on both sides by the blank whitewashed or painted walls of the buildings. Heavy wooden doors opened directly onto the street. Here and there a glimmer of light showed in an upstairs window.

Grofield stopped two blocks away, in a patch of darkness against a doorway, and studied the terrain. Ahead of him on the right there was a Volkswagen Microbus with Mexican plates, parked facing downhill. In the next block there was an elderly Ford with Texas plates, parked on the left facing uphill, and across from it a motorcycle was leaning against a yellow wall. In the block after that, away from any streetlight, was the rented Datsun.

No one was in sight.

Grofield, studying it, decided one of the three might be in or next to the Ford, another would be hidden somewhere on the downhill side of the Datsun, and the third would probably be either in the Datsun itself or in a doorway right handy to it.

First things first. The Ford.

Grofield looked at the narrow blank street, trying to work out an approach to the Ford, and from behind him came a sudden burst of conversation. He turned his head, and coming down toward him was a group of three couples, all elderly, talking away with great animation. Grofield waited, and when they got to him he smiled and said, "Good evening."

They were surprised, but said good evening back to him. To keep them from stopping, Grofield fell into step with them, in the middle of their group, saying, "This is my first day in San Miguel. I think it's great."

They all agreed it was great. Now that the surprise was over, they were all obviously pleased at his interruption; he afforded a touch of the unexpected to their night on the town. They were permanent residents, they said; each couple rented a house somewhere in town. They told him how cheaply a whole house could be rented—fifty dollars a month, forty dollars a month.

They asked him where he was from, and when he told them, they all began to talk about people they knew or had known from New York.

At the Ford, Grofield stopped abruptly and said, "Well, good night."

"Good night," they said. He'd stopped so suddenly the group had gone on a pace or two without realizing it, so he was already separated from them. They paused to wave, to finish sentences, and then moved on. Grofield opened the car door, showed the Beretta to the guy crouched on the floor in there, and said, genially, "Just think of the mess it would make."

All cramped up like that, having hidden down there out of sight when he'd seen the group of senior citizens coming, he hadn't had a chance to get at whatever armament he might have been toting himself. He stared sullenly at the gun in Grofield's fist and said nothing.

It wasn't Honner himself, but one of the others, the guy Elly had slugged. Grofield said to him, "What if this had been their car? Those old people? What then?"

The guy kept on looking sullen.

"Oh, well. Okay, come on out of there."

The guy put one forearm on the seat, reached the other hand up to the steering wheel, and heaved himself upward into the descending path of the Beretta. The butt caught him on the temple and he sagged back down onto the floor again, his mouth hanging open.

Grofield, putting the gun away and crawling into the car, muttered, "One thing you can say for your job, you get a lot of rest time." Moving with difficulty in the narrow space, he removed one of the guy's shoelaces and used it to tie his thumbs together behind his back. Lying the way he was, all cramped up and with his arms useless, it was unlikely he'd get out of the car under his own steam. He was like a turtle on his back.

Grofield left the Ford cautiously, looked around for activity, saw none, and walked back uphill to the first cross street. He turned right, hurried over to the next block, turned right, down a block, right again, and came back to the street he'd initially left. The Ford was now uphill to his right, the Datsun just around the corner to his left.

There was no point worrying about the guy stationed downhill. The thing to do was clear the one near the car, which was parked facing uphill anyway, then get into the car fast and up the hill, pick up Elly, and get the hell out of town before Honner and the others could get themselves organized.

So where was number two? Grofield approached the intersection cautiously, peeked around the corner, and there he was. Sitting on a doorstep directly across the street from the car, smoking a cigarette, looking idle and harmless. He could take a chance on sitting out there in the open like that because he was a new face; Grofield had never seen him before.

Did that mean there were four of them now?

No, it was more likely this was a replacement for the one they'd given the shock treatment. He was maybe not yet in condition for round two.

But that Honner could replace him this fast, in Mexico City, was bad news. That he could do so meant Grofield could no longer be sure exactly how much manpower he was up against. Had it just been Honner and two other guys who'd checked the car-rental agencies and found out where he and the girl had gone, or did Honner have an unlimited supply of assistants?

Once again, Grofield wished he knew more about what was going on here, what Elly had herself involved in.

All right. Later. Right now, there was a new boy to be initiated. And in order to do it, Grofield had to walk all over the county, retracing his steps around the block and then going around the block on the far side so as to come back to this intersection from the opposite direction. He got there at last, peeked around the corner, and the new boy was just to his right, about ten feet away, still smoking and lazing and looking like local color. Except that the face came off the Brooklyn docks.

Grofield stuck his head around the corner and said, "Psst!"

The guy looked up, startled.

Grofield showed him the Beretta. "You stand up slow," he said softly, "and come around here for a get-acquainted chat."

The guy said, "I don't know what you're up to, buddy. You got me mistaken for somebody else."

"Oh no," Grofield told him. "If I had you mistaken for somebody else, you wouldn't know it. You'd think this was a holdup. To plead ignorance before the question has been asked is to reveal knowledge. Confucius says. Come on around the corner, honey, it's hazing time for the new pledges."

The guy looked disgusted. He flicked away his cigarette—would that have been a signal to somebody?—and got to his feet and came around the corner, where Grofield hit him twice with the Beretta. Twice because the guy rolled with it the first time.

And now Grofield was in a hurry. Honner was probably staked out downhill somewhere, and had surely seen his boy walk around the corner. He'd be coming to see what was what.

Grofield came charging out from the cross street, unlocked the Datsun, jumped in, and was just putting the key in the ignition when he heard the scream.

7

GROFIELD SQUEALED the Datsun around the square, and suddenly they were right in front of him, frozen in the glare of the headlights, a tableau straight off the cover of a 1940 pulp magazine. Against a background of cobblestone street and dark old buildings, the slender blonde struggled in the grip of two men, two burly types in dark clothing. One of them was Honner, the other was a second new face.

Grofield braked hard, stuck the Beretta out the window, and fired into the air, at the same time shouting, "Elly! Get over here!"

The new man let go of Elly and ran for cover, out of range of the headlights. Honner, not giving up so easily, kept holding onto Elly until she kicked him three or four times, when he too let go. Elly dashed for the car.

With her out of the way, Grofield snapped two quick shots at Honner, neither of which seemed to score. Honner, ducking low and fumbling inside his coat for a weapon of his own, ran away to the right toward the row of parked cars.

Elly scrambled into the car, and Grofield had tromped down on the accelerator before she was fully in. Her door slammed, she said, "Wow!" and they careened on around the square and down the hill, headed for the road out of town.

She tried to talk a couple of times, but was too out of breath, so she just sat there, half-turned so she could look back out the rear window. Grofield drove the way the Datsun people had never intended.

After a while he said, "You've got to tell me what I'm up

against. I can't work blind like this; I make mistakes I don't know about."

"What mistakes?" She was still somewhat out of breath, but better. "You did fine," she said.

"Sure I did. I figured the three we knew were all there was, so it was safe to leave you and go for the guys on plant around the car. But there were two new faces back there, honey, two of them."

"Don't get mad at me, Alan, please."

"You damn fool."

"Please."

Now that they were safe again for the moment, Grofield's irritation was growing like Topsy. "What have you got me up against, damn it? A whole army?"

"No. Not an army, honest."

"What, then?"

"I wish I could tell you," she said. "Maybe I can Friday, when this is all over."

"It may be over a lot sooner than Friday," he said.

She took a quick look out the rear window, but there was no other traffic on the road. "Why?" she said. "They can't follow us now."

"I'm not talking about them, I'm talking about us."

"You mean, you'll walk out on me."

"Walk, hell, I'll run. I'd fly if I could."

"This afternoon you—"

"This afternoon we wound up in bed. Which we both had known would happen since the first minute we looked at one another. It had nothing to do with anything else. You didn't climb into my bed as part of a contract for me to stay with you till Friday, and I didn't service you in order to keep you with me either."

"Service!"

"That's the word for it."

"You can be a first-class grade-A bastard when you want, can't you?"

"You send me in to fight three guys and I'm up against the goddamn Light Brigade. Don't talk about bastards."

She folded her arms, demonstrating a czarist contempt, and stared out the side window.

They drove the rest of the way to the hotel in silence.

As they were getting out of the car she said, "You know, *I* rented this car. If we split up, it goes with me."

"Take it with my blessing. You can drop me off at the first city we come to."

"I'll drop you off right here, you mean."

"Don't get smart-ass, Ellen Marie."

"You're a hateful man. You're the most hateful man I ever met."

He walked away from her, went to his room, and unlocked the door. Inside, he left the door open and started to pack. He had the keys to the Datsun in his pocket, so he wasn't worried about her taking off without him.

The other two guns and the three wallets were in his new suitcase. He took the usable papers from the wallets, threw the wallets in the wastebasket, stowed the papers in a pocket of the suitcase, and put the two extra guns in the pockets of his new raincoat. Then he packed everything else, leaving the raincoat out to be carried separately.

She came into the room as he was shutting the lid. "I'm sorry," she said.

He looked at her, and she was being the little girl again, this time practically Baby Snooks. "Sorry again?" he asked her. "It must be a rough life, being sorry for this and that all the time."

"But I am sorry," she said. She came over and sat down on the bed. "I was just upset, because of those men grabbing me and all."

"You're about as trustworthy," he told her, "as a pool shark. Cut out the innocent and frightened bit, I'm wise to you."

"I'm not faking, Alan, honest I'm not. I *am* innocent, in some ways, and you can bet your bottom dollar I'm frightened."

"And you can bet *your* bottom dollar we're through."

"Alan—"

"All up," he said.

The little girl turned on a little sex. "Please?"

"Kaput," he said. He picked up the two suitcases. "Better get your stuff into the car. They'll be out here looking for us sooner or later."

"Alan, please."

He left the room, went over to the car, and stuffed his luggage onto the back seat. Then he stood beside the car, waiting.

She came over without her bags. "It's a beautiful night," she said.

"Oh, bushwah. Will you cut it out?"

"If those two hadn't jumped me, we wouldn't be fighting, would we? We'd have come back here and had that moonlight swim—there is a moon, did you even notice it?—and then—"

"Yeah, there's a moon," he said. "A nice thin sliver. And a great big pool full of warm water. And a darling bed. And neither one of us would last till Friday, because you don't have brains enough to let me know what's going on so I can tell what to do about it."

"Alan—"

"I leave here in two minutes," he said, looking at his watch. "With you or without you."

"Alan, I *want* to tell you!"

He stood silent, ostentatiously following the sweep second hand of his watch.

"We can keep away from them now. Mexico's a big country, we can go wherever we want, they'll never find us."

He ignored her.

"We had a bargain," she said.

"It's off."

"Alan, please!"

"One minute," he said. "Better get your bags."

"How could you be sure I was telling you the truth? How do you know I wouldn't just lie to you again?"

He looked up from the watch. "If it sounds like a lie," he said, "I'll ditch you. And I think I can tell when you're lying to me. I've seen better liars."

She waved her arms in a helpless gesture. "All right," she said. "I'll tell you."

8

"I DON'T KNOW where to begin," she said, looking gloomily at the dashboard.

Grofield glanced away from the road. "That sounds like the preamble to a non-truth," he said. "Watch it."

"Oh, I'll tell the truth," she said. "Don't worry about that." She sounded fatalistic, the last defenses gone.

They were on the road, heading north. Rather than wait around at the hotel while listening to whatever she was going to have to say to him, Grofield had had her get her luggage and stow it away, and now they were moving again. She could tell him her story while he drove.

He'd taken a quick look at the road map, and decided to make for San Luis Potosí, a medium-size city about a hundred twenty-five miles away. They'd take this secondary road north to Dolores Hidalgo, then another secondary road back out to the main highway, Route 57 again, and then straight north to San Luis Potosí.

Now, as they drove along, she was supposed to be telling him at last what was going on, but after the doubtful preamble, she stayed glum and silent, gazing at the dashboard.

"The last I heard from you," he said, to prompt her, "you didn't know where to begin."

"I was just trying to get it all straight in my head," she said. She looked at him, her expression somber in the light from the dashboard. "I hope you really can tell when I'm lying and when I'm not lying, because I'm terribly afraid this is going to sound like the biggest lie of all."

"Try me."

"All right." She took a deep breath, and said, "The best place to start, I guess, is with Governor Harrison. Governor Luke Harrison, of Pennsylvania. He used to be governor, a few years ago, but the title sticks."

"That's our lead character, then," Grofield said. "Governor Luke Harrison of Pennsylvania."

"I'm not telling you a lie!"

"What?" He glanced at her, and she was clearly upset. Looking back at the road he said, "Oh, you mean because I said lead character? I meant nothing by that, I was only using trade idiom. Remember, by profession I'm an actor."

"An actor? You mean, for real?"

"Let's not lose the thread, honey, I'll show you my scrapbook later. We were, when last seen, studying a close-up of Governor Luke Harrison. Of Pennsylvania."

"Yes. I . . . I'd better tell you about him, something about the way he is, so you'll understand the rest of it."

"By all means."

"He's one of the richest men in the state, in the first place, maybe the richest. He owns mines, and he's in steel production, and his family has owned a lot of property around Philadelphia since before the Civil War."

"Money *and* social status?"

"If he wanted it, yes. He's what Philadelphia calls Main Line."

"I know that. The New York equivalent is, or used to be, the Four Hundred."

"Yes. But the thing is, he inherited all of it, the money and the position and everything. And he's a dynamic man, a forceful man, he's . . . he's almost frightening to be near, there's so much energy in him, so much drive."

"You know him personally, then."

There was the faintest of hesitations, and then, in a flat voice she said, "Yes."

"All right. A dynamo with inherited money and social position. The way that usually runs, the guy goes into politics just to work off the excess energy. He can afford to be a liberal, because they're taxing him at ninety-one percent anyway, and the consciousness of the stuff that he got on a silver platter makes him one of those forthright fighters for the common man. Raise the minimum wage, increase unemployment insurance, give more aid to education, it's up to government to solve the problems and make the world more beautiful."

"Perfect," she said. "That's exactly the kind of man he was. Is."

"I'll do you another one," Grofield told her. "In the old days, when government changed hands, it went back and forth between the machine boss and the reform group. Thirty years of the machine, two years of reform, thirty years of the same old machine, and so on. But not anymore. These days, it goes back and forth between the economizers and the social workers. I'll bet your boy took over from a guy whose boast was that he'd balanced the state budget."

She smiled, though reluctantly. "Right again," she said. "And lost the next election to a man who promised to cut state taxes. Did you guess all that, or did you used to live in Pennsylvania?"

"Wherever I live, I take no interest in politics. Except in the abstract, of course. Shall we get back to the story?"

"Yes." She smiled again, wanly, and said, "You don't know how much I'd rather not talk about it. But if I must— For God's sake, Alan, don't ever use this. Don't ever say anything to anybody, don't ever—"

"Scout's honor. The story."

"All right. Back to Governor Harrison. He only had the one term as governor, and then he tried to turn a favorite-son Presidential nomination into a real nomination. It didn't work, and he got a lot of the bigwigs in the party sore at him, so when he wanted to run for Senator from Pennsylvania, he didn't get the nomination."

"Many are called, but few are chosen."

The comment, tossed off as a glib space-filler, seemed to intrigue her. "Do you think so? Maybe you're right, maybe that's what it is."

"I have the feeling," he said, in order to get her back on the track, "that Governor Luke Harrison isn't ready to retire, and is still struggling for public office somewhere. Mayor of Philadelphia?"

"Oh, no. He has too much pride for that, he can't possibly take any job smaller than what he's already had."

"So he's moved out of politics into something else."

"Not exactly. For the last several years he hasn't done much of anything. He's run charity funds and so on, he was involved in some sort of educational organization for the UN, he had an advisory post in Washington for a while, but nothing full, nothing solid, nothing to use up all his interest and energy."

"Description of a powder keg," said Grofield.

She nodded. "Yes. About to explode."

"Now we get to you."

"Not yet. There are other people in this. Governor Harrison's son Bob. He's twenty-nine years old, and for the past seven years he's been personal press secretary to General Pozos."

She'd said that last name as though she assumed Grofield would recognize it, but he didn't. "General Pozos? Never had the pleasure."

"Oh, you must have heard of him. He's the dictator of Guerrero."

"Strike two."

"Really? It's a country in Central America. You've never heard of it?"

"If I have, I don't remember. But all right, I'll take your word for it. General Pozos is dictator of Guerrero. Is that what they call him? Dictator?"

"Oh no. Officially he's *El Presidente*. There was an election and everything. In 1937. And any year now, as soon as they get the constitution ready, there'll be new elections and the provisional government will be replaced by a permanent democratic government."

"Since 1937."

"Yes."

Grofield nodded. "They don't like to rush into things."

"Haste makes waste."

"Right. Back on the beam, now. So far, we've got Governor

Harrison in Pennsylvania, full of energy and out of work. We've got his son doing what?"

"Press secretary. Public relations, that means. Trying to get the General a better press in the United States, mostly."

"Check. The son is a PR man in Latin America. So now we have a cast of two, father and son."

"Three. General Pozos."

"Oh? He fits in here, too?"

"He's the middle of it."

"Any more characters, or do we get to the plot now?"

"More characters. Only one more to know about now. General Pozos has a son, too. Juan. He's twenty-one years old, and he's a senior at the University of Pennsylvania."

"Aha. The two sons have switched countries."

"Yes. Juan has been in the United States for eight years, since he started high school. Summertimes he spends back in Guerrero. Christmas and Thanksgiving and Easter he spends with Governor Harrison. The Governor met General Pozos about twelve years ago, when they were both in Washington, and when it came time to send Juan north for his education, the Governor offered to take the boy into his own house. Bob was twenty-one then, just leaving home, and Juan, I guess, was a sort of substitute son for him."

"So far," Grofield said, "I don't seem to catch a glimpse of Honner and the boys, and Acapulco seems far away."

"All right, I'm getting to it. I have more to tell you about Governor Harrison, but believe me, it's all necessary if you're going to understand what's happening now."

Grofield sighed, and shrugged his shoulders. "Carry on," he said. But at the same time he wasn't as impatient as he sounded; this variety of personnel, this wealth of detail and fullness of background, were indications of truth. He believed this story, or would as soon as she started to tell it; lies have a clearer and more sensible line.

"Several years ago," she said, "the Governor bought a house in Santo Stefano, that's the capital city of Guerrero. He spends his summers there, spends a few days now and then the rest of the year. He's gotten interested in Guerrero, in the country's economy, its resources, its potential, its people, its history, just everything about it."

"Ahhh. A little country all his own. The kind of man you're talking about would like that."

"He more than likes it," she said. "He has an obsession for it."

Grofield glanced at her. She was serious, intense, level-eyed; her cheekbones were prominent, casting shadows in the small light from the dashboard. He said, low-voiced, "I believe we're getting to it now."

"Yes. Governor Harrison wants Guerrero. He wants to run it himself, create a true nation of it. With General Pozos running things, the Governor can't do much, but for eight years he's been the most important single person in the life of General Pozos' son Juan. When the General dies and Juan takes over—and he will, that's guaranteed—*then* Governor Harrison can have Guerrero to himself. With Juan as the figurehead, with his own son Bob to handle the public relations and the paperwork, Governor Harrison can take the raw materials of a nation into his hands and do whatever he wants with it."

"King Luke the First."

But she shook her head. "No. He doesn't want glory, he doesn't want privilege. He doesn't even want power, not for himself. He was born with all of that. What Governor Harrison wants is to serve the people. I've heard him talk, Alan, I've listened to him talk about this very thing, and he *means* it. He wants to raise the standard of living in Guerrero, wants to get good schools, good housing, good everything. He isn't fooling, and he isn't kidding himself. And if he gets the chance to do what he wants, it *will* be better for the people of Guerrero. In ten years he could make it the most advanced nation in Central America, maybe in Central and South America both. And right now it has the next to the lowest standard of living of any nation in the Western Hemisphere."

"So he's a good man."

"No. He wants to do good things, but he's not a good man. He's—you've got to understand this, he's had this dream in his mind for years now, years and years. And the way General Pozos lives—it would take Charles Laughton to do a movie biography of him—and the age he is, nearly sixty, it just seems as though it can't be long to wait. But the years go by, and General Pozos keeps on living, and Governor Harrison has to keep on waiting."

"I think I see it coming."

"Of course. And Juan is graduating from college this year. The Governor wanted him to stay on, to do postgraduate work, but Juan said no. He's going to move back to Guerrero, he'll live there permanently. And very soon the Governor won't control him anymore. Juan will be left to himself, and he might even grow up to be his own man."

"The Governor can't afford to wait."

"No. And he realizes what he plans to do is evil, but he believes there are extenuating circumstances. The General is himself more evil than any single act against him could be, that's one argument. And the ultimate good for all the people of Guerrero is more important than the immediate evil of the act, that's another. And for a third, in a truly civilized world the General would have been executed for his crimes long ago, so this is merely the commission of an overdue *good* act."

Grofield grinned. "I must ask the Governor to do all my rationalizing for me."

"He's good at it, mostly because he *believes* so completely himself." She hesitated, as though at the brink of something, some dark pit, and then said, in a lower tone. "And he can convince other people, too. He's a forceful man, a dominant man."

"In other words, he isn't doing the job himself. He's talked someone else into doing it."

"Yes."

Grofield waited, but she didn't say anything, so finally he said, "Who?"

"A doctor," she said. "His own personal physician. When the Governor is running Guerrero, this doctor will run the Ministry of Health, will establish the hospitals and clinics, will even form a medical school. The two of them have talked about it for years together, the doctor's as caught up in it as Governor Harrison, he even has architectural drawings of hospitals, he has lists of names of men he would try to hire away from American hospitals and universities."

"Their own private model-train layout."

"Yes! Yes! *That's* what's wrong with it, neither of them cares about the *people!* The populace, yes, but not the people, not the individual men and women. It's just a population, and buildings, and land area, and natural resources, and harbors, and rivers . . ."

Grofield prodded slightly, saying, "Anyway, the doctor is going to do the job himself."

"Yes. General Pozos is not a healthy man. He couldn't be, the life he leads. This doctor has cared for him from time to time in the past, and now he's volunteered to go down there and be the General's personal physician on a full-time basis. The General, of course, thinks that's wonderful."

"What's the plan? Accident?"

"Oh, no. Just bad health. General Pozos will waste away, will have this and that with complications. He won't last three months. A personal physician, in constant daily contact with the patient, can kill in a thousand different ways."

Grofield said, "Oh." He turned on the car heater. "This plan is new," he said.

"Brand-new. The General is on his yacht now, he's spending two weeks cruising up and down the Pacific coast. He'll be at sea until Friday morning, when he'll come to land—"

"At Acapulco."

"Yes. Mexico has separate states, you know, the same as we do, and Acapulco is in the state of Guerrero."

"The same name as the country."

"Right. So the General makes frequent stops there, for a day, two days, just long enough to pick out one or two women in bathing suits. He makes a production out of it, how the peoples of the two Guerreros, nation and state, are hand in hand in eternal friendship and all that. He makes a speech, usually, and has an official luncheon. The people at Acapulco like it fine, because Acapulco is a resort town, and colorful ceremonies about celebrities are always welcome in a resort town."

Grofield said, "And you, knowing about the plan, have decided to go down to Acapulco on Friday and warn the General to be on the eary."

"On the what?"

"On the eary. It's slang, don't worry about it, it means to be careful."

"Oh. Yes, that's what I want to do."

"Whereas Governor Harrison, aware of your intention, has hired Honner to stop you. Honner has a blank check and can hire however many goons it takes."

"Yes. Honner's a private detective in Philadelphia. Or at least that's what he calls himself. He's done the Governor's dirty work before."

Grofield watched the road, a two-lane blacktop, straight as a die. Rolling, semiarid countryside stretched away on both sides, virtually lifeless. Every once in a great while there would be a small lone flickering light out in the darkness to left or right; a candle showing through the glassless window of a solitary mud hut. A smoke-snorting truck or a rushing passenger car would go by every now and again, headed south, at intervals of about ten minutes. It was bleak, poor, dry, empty country, with no towns or diners or roadside stands, no crossroads or gas stations or taverns. A bad place, particularly if Honner and his boys caught up.

Grofield looked in the rearview mirror and couldn't be sure it was angled right, because he couldn't see anything in it, only blackness. He twisted quickly around in the seat, holding the wheel with his left hand, and looked out the back window, and the mirror had reported the truth; there was about a foot of visible road behind the car, glowing dull red in the illumination of the taillights, but beyond that, stretching back to the edge of the world and over, there was nothing. Emptiness, blackness, darkness, and blind nothing.

Grofield faced front again.

Beside him, she looked back, then front, saying, "What's the matter?"

"Nothing. I'm thinking."

He was thinking about her story. He believed it, both for what she'd said and for the way she'd said it. There had been hesitations here and there in the recital that led him to believe he didn't yet have the whole truth, but he was convinced that what he'd been told was at least part of it.

But there were still questions. He asked one of them: "You're taking a lot of trouble, you're risking your neck. Are you sure it's worth it?"

"What?"

"Why try to save General Pozos' life at the risk of your own? If he's such a bastard, why sweat it?"

"Because he's a human being. Because no man should take another man's life, that's anarchy, that's—"

"Okay, okay, okay." He was about to hear a judge-not-lest-ye-be-judged speech, and he would rather not. He said, "What's the General to you? What's the relationship between you?"

"We've met, that's all. Hello, how are you, lovely weather. At receptions, places like that."

"Then where's your connection with all this? You know all the inside dope, you've heard the Governor talk about what he's going to do with Guerrero, where do you come in? You the Governor's daughter?"

"No. The doctor's."

Grofield looked at her, and saw her wide-eyed and solemn. He turned his eyes back to the road. "Big Ed Fitzgerald?"

"Doctor Edgar Fitzgerald. He's what they call an eminent physician. He's my father."

"And he knows about Honner and—"

"Oh no. I knew something was going on, and I knew Dad was troubled, and he finally told me what they were planning to do. What *he* was planning to do. I tried to talk him out of it, I tried to, tried to get him to *think* about it, *see* it, under*stand* what he's planning to do, but he's blinded by visions of good works, the greater good for the greater number—"

"The end justifies the means."

She smiled bitterly. She said, "He told me the Bible said that twice, once for and once against. It says the end doesn't justify the means, but it also says by their fruits ye shall know them, meaning that good fruit has to come from a good tree, meaning the end justifies the means."

"He's buried his conscience in a ton of soft, round words."

"Liberally sprinkled with ideals."

"How do we get from your father to Honner?"

"I told him I would warn General Pozos when he got to Acapulco. You know, I don't know of any way to get to him before that, he's just out there in the Pacific someplace with a lot of whores. So I threatened to go to Acapulco, and he tried locking me away in my room, but I got away. So then I suppose he told the Governor, and I can just see it. The Governor calming him down, talking to him in that good, low, *confidential* voice of his, putting his hand around my father's shoulders, saying, 'Don't you worry, Ed, we'll find your little girl, we'll keep her safe.' And then telling Honner, 'Find the little bitch, I don't care what it costs. Don't let her get to Pozos.' And when Honner wants to know where the line is drawn, the Governor smiles at him and says, 'Use your discretion.' That's his line, that's the way you get evil things done for a good purpose. You hire a man and tell him what the good purpose is, and when he asks you how to get that good purpose you say to him, 'Use your discretion.' And this time it means, keep her alive if you possibly can, but the main thing is not to let her talk to General Pozos."

"But what if they decide they have to kill you? What's your father going to do then?"

"Nothing. He won't know about it. They'll cover it somehow, I'll just disappear, nobody knows where I am. Oh, she's off pouting somewhere, that's all, she'll turn up. And after the General's dead, what does it matter?"

"Mm." Grofield thought. "I have one more question."

"All right."

"Why did you come to bed with me? I thought it was a bribe, at least partly, to keep me with you, but that doesn't figure now. You wouldn't use that kind of a bribe to save General Pozos, he's the wrong kind of Holy Grail to sacrifice yourself for."

She smiled. "You should have a higher opinion of yourself."

"I do. I also thought it was a bribe you got change on, and that you knew it."

"Hah! Look out you don't get round-shouldered from hugging yourself. You want a cigarette?"

"Yes. I also want an answer."

"I'll answer, don't worry." She lit two cigarettes, holding both in her mouth at the same time walrus-like, handed one to him, blew a cloud of smoke, and said, "I suppose partly it was reaction. We were safe, or at least we thought we were, and I was grateful, and the urgency was over for the moment. You know, it's a well-known psychological fact that people think about sex right after a narrow escape. Preservation of the species, or something."

"People *think* about sex all the time. I want to know why you did something about it."

"Well, that's part of it. And also, as I said, gratitude. And maybe a bribe, too, a little bit. And mostly . . ." she gave him a crooked smile and a warm look ". . . mostly curiosity."

"Did you find out?"

"Mmmm."

Grofield grinned. "Think there might be more to learn?"

"I don't know. Ask me when we get wherever we're going."

"San Luis Potosí. The ruby in the forehead of Old May-hee-co."

She waved the hand holding the cigarette, a careless gesture. "Olé," she said.

9

"THE WAY I see it," Grofield said, scratching his head and studying the map, "we can bypass Mexico City and go through a place called Toluca instead, on something called Route 55, and take that down to Taxco, but from Taxco on there's only the one road to Acapulco, and Honner's going to be all over that road like a white line."

They were sitting together on the terrace outside their hotel room. San Luis Potasí, a cramped, old picturesque city of narrow streets and Old World buildings, was spread out before them like the Spanish section of Paris in a musical by MGM. They had come here Wednesday night, and now it was nine o'clock Thursday morning, time to be leaving. Bright sunlight shone on the map spread out on the table in front of them, their breakfast dishes pushed to one side. The used coffee cups were taking on a cargo of cigarette butts.

She said, "There has to be another way, Alan. Can't we go straight to the ocean from here, and then along the coast? What's wrong with that? Look, we go from here to Aguascalientes to Guadalajara to Colima to Tecomán on the coast."

"Sure," he said. "And then look. An unimproved road as far as Aquila, and then nothing."

"What's that dotted line, from Aquila to—what is it? Playa Azul."

He looked at the legend, said, "Proposed road. They haven't built it yet."

"Couldn't we do it anyway? Maybe we could rent a jeep, it's probably just sand along there—"

"It could also be jungle. Besides, that dotted line crosses two rivers, honey, and I guarantee you it does it a lot easier than we could."

"Well, damn!" She stubbed out another cigarette in a coffee cup, and immediately lit a fresh one. "There's got to be a way."

"Trains and planes are out," he said. "They'll be blanketing the terminals, we wouldn't get as far as the sidewalk. We've got to try it by car, that's all there is to it. We shouldn't have any trouble getting as far as Taxco, but after that it might be trouble."

"*Might* be!"

"All right, will be. But we've got to try it."

She bent over the map again. "What if we went around to the other side and down to the coast and back up? Isn't there any road there either?"

"Nope. Look."

She looked, and there was nothing, and she kept on looking, and there kept on being nothing. Finally she sat up and said, "All right, I give up. We have to drive to Acapulco, and we have to take the only road, and I don't see how we're going to get there."

"What we'll do," he said, "is drive as far as Taxco, and then scout the territory. We can't make plans of our own until we know how they're set up. And they've got to be south of Taxco, because there's three different roads we could be on until you get a few miles south of Taxco at, what is it, at Iguala. There's no point in their watching three roads when they can wait a few miles farther south and only have to watch one road."

"All right. But I'm not hopeful."

"I am," he said. "Aside from everything else, if this all works out, it'll take care of a little problem of my own."

"What problem?"

"I'm in this country illegally. I've got no papers, nothing. That'll make it a little tough for me to get back *out* of the country without drawing attention to myself. If you manage to get to General Pozos, and if you manage to convince him you're telling the truth, then the General is liable to be grateful to you and consider he owes you a favor. And the favor can be to rig some diplomatic courier route for me to sneak back into the States. Sensible?"

She smiled. "Good," she said. "Self-interest always helps people perform at their best."

"Is that right? You're being a smart-ass again, you know that?"

She squinted at him. "Are you really married?"

"Yes."

"Shouldn't you telephone your wife, or send her a telegram, or something?"

"No. I told her I'd be gone for a while, and she knows the kind of work I'm in, so she doesn't expect to hear from me till she sees me."

"*I* don't know the kind of work you're in."

"You're not married to me."

She sat back, studying him, and said, "Some day I'd like to fill you full of truth serum and sit you down in front of a tape recorder and have you reel off your full life story. I bet it's got some pretty odd moments in it."

"Only since I met up with you. You done with that coffee?"

She looked into the cup at all the soggy butts. "Ugh! Are you kidding?"

"Then let's go." He folded up the map.

She said, "Shall we synchronize our watches?"

"After we put on blackface."

"Yes, sir, Mister Interlocutor."

Grofield laughed and said, "You're a lot of fun, Elly, my dear. Too bad you're about to get killed."

10

GROFIELD WALKED down a street lined on both sides with tourist shops selling goods made of silver—Taxco was the silver center of Mexico, besides being its other city-size national monument—and at the corner he found a taxi, a dilapidated old Chevrolet with a heavy bear of a man at the wheel. Grofield stuck his head in the side window and said, "I want to go for a ride. Out of town."

The driver turned his head and looked at him, like a man with nothing in this world but time and patience. "Where to?"

"A round trip. Down through Iguala and down the road toward Acapulco. A few miles. And then back here again."

The driver turned it over, turned it over, and said, "Ten pesos."

Eighty cents. Grofield said, "Sold." He opened the back door and climbed aboard.

Slowly, with a constant shifting of gears, the driver pushed his Chevrolet southward out of town.

Grofield sat back, adjusting his sunglasses on his nose. Back in town, Elly was waiting in a tourist restaurant, her blond hair covered by a white bandanna. The Datsun was parked on a side street, where it was less likely to be noticed. Not that there was much to worry about there, anyway. Since Mexico had no make of car of its own, all of its automobiles were imported, with a minority of them being the expensive, big cars from the United States. The smaller, cheaper Datsun was a very popular car around here and less noticeable than a Plymouth or Ford. Also, because of the bleaching quality of the tropic sun, light colors were the rule; a cream-colored Datsun was anonymity itself.

"Drive slow," Grofield said, when they cleared town. "I'm looking for friends of mine."

"Sure. You know, I used to drive a hack in the States. In New York City."

Grofield didn't answer that at all; he couldn't afford the distraction of a nice chat.

The set of the driver's shoulders, the heaviness of his silence, showed he was offended.

The road skirted Iguala to the east, and a mile or so further hooked up with the main road between Mexico City and Acapulco. From here north it was a toll road, but southward to Acapulco it was free. Since Taxco the road had been all downhill, but now it leveled. They were still high on a plateau, and ahead of them, southward, Grofield could see the bulky mountains between here and the sea.

"Slowly, now," said Grofield. "My friends should be along here somewhere."

There were virtually no roads in Mexico more than two lanes wide, including the main highways, and this one was no exception. It was straight and flat at the moment, but narrow. Hilly, cultivated land flanked the road on both sides, and there were a last few buildings, bars, and restaurants. The government gas station, Pemex, had been back at the crossroads.

Grofield nearly missed it when he came to it. The dark green Pontiac, back in condition again, apparently, and parked in the shade beside a broken-down, roofless mud shack off the right side of the road. Grofield saw it out of the corner of his eye, sat back in the cab seat, and waited while they went on by. Then he watched out the rear window until he was sure they hadn't noticed him—they weren't looking for *him*, they were looking for her, or for both of them together—and then he leaned forward and said to the driver, "Okay, that's fine. We can go back now."

"I thought you were looking for friends."

"They aren't here yet."

The driver shrugged and turned the car around. Going past the second time, Grofield could see Honner and three other guys sitting under a stunted tree near the car. They could take it easy and wait. They knew they had a faster car than Grofield and Elly, and faster than anything else they might have rented instead of the Datsun. All Honner and his boys had to do was sit there in the shade and watch the traffic, which was sparse, anyway, and when their quarry went by they could slowly get to their feet, brush their trousers off, stroll to their Pontiac, catch up with the Datsun and run it off the road—and the game would be over.

Except, Grofield assured himself, that it wasn't going to be quite that easy.

On the way back to Taxco, winding and uphill, Grofield tried belatedly to get the driver into conversation about the old days hacking in New York, but it was too late. The driver's feelings were hurt, and he wouldn't talk. They were both relieved to get back to town and separate from one another.

Grofield found Elly sitting over a cup of cold coffee, chain-smoking again. He sat down and said, "I spotted them. They don't expect us this early, but they're there just in case."

"So what do we do now?"

"Go back to that motel we saw, take a room, and wait."

"Till when?"

"I figure about three o'clock in the morning would be about right."

She shivered. "What a thought."

"Let's hope it doesn't occur to Honner."

11

"I'LL BE BACK as quick as I can," Grofield said.

"Good."

He shut the car door, making the interior light go off, and now they were in darkness. He stood up, putting one hand on the car to keep himself oriented, and waited for his eyes to accustom themselves to the night, but they didn't seem to want to do it. The sliver of moon was even thinner tonight, and there was no artificial light anywhere in the world.

The time was three-thirty in the morning, and the Datsun was on the dirt beside the road just a little way north of the shack where Grofield had seen the Pontiac. They hadn't seen another car since they left Taxco. They might as well have been standing on a rock in the asteroid belt.

After a while Grofield could begin vaguely to make out the difference between the flat, straight roadway and the less-black, less-even countryside. He moved away from the car, out onto the blacktop, and walked slowly along, keeping to the silence of the blacktop and off the soft crunching of the roadside dirt.

He was weighted down with equipment. The Beretta was in one hip pocket, and a small bottle of gasoline was in the other. A foldaway knife was in his left-side trouser pocket, a torn-off strip of T-shirt and some matches were in the right side, and he carried another sock-and-soap blackjack in his left hand. He was, he hoped, ready for whatever came up.

Ahead of him there was a faint flicker of light. He moved toward it, cautiously, hoping some late-night driver wouldn't pick this moment to go tearing by, all noise and wind and bright headlights. But the blackness remained silent and empty, and Grofield moved slowly through it toward the flickering light.

It came from the roofless shack. Grofield approached, cautious and silent, as in his head he heard background music, movie music; and he was an Apache creeping up on the wagon train, slow and silent with the deadly stealth of the red man, that lore of the forest that . . .

They had a table in there, with a candle on it. They had folding chairs, and three of them were sitting around playing cards, Honner and two others. The fourth guy was nowhere to be seen.

Grofield worked his way around the shack to the Pontiac, and was almost to it when he heard the voices. He stopped, startled, and listened.

There were two guys in the Pontiac, talking together idly, the way people do when they're bored and waiting and they've run out of all the good anecdotes. That made five, one more than this afternoon.

No, six. The sixth one came walking along, a flashlight beam ahead of him, emerging suddenly out of the darkness. Grofield crouched behind the Pontiac, waiting and listening.

The newcomer, with the flashlight, said, "Okay, time's up. You get out there for a while."

"You ask me, they ain't coming this way."

"That's okay. It's your turn to get out by the road."

"Marty, come along with me, keep me company."

A third voice—the other one who'd been in the car to begin with—said, "The hell with that. It's cold out there."

They mumbled and groused among themselves a minute or two more, and then the changeover of the guard was made, and the new man on duty went shambling away with the flashlight, leaving this area in darkness again, while the two now in the car lit cigarettes and picked up the threads of an old conversation.

There were two cars. In the dim side glow of the flashlight, Grofield had seen the other one, parked just to the right. A Mercedes-Benz 230SL, the fast sports car.

It must have been further down the road this afternoon, when he'd come around looking. If he'd taken out the Pontiac then, and gone blithely on through, this Mercedes would have gobbled him up two or three miles down the road. But now they'd all come together to live through the grim Mexican night.

Grofield took out the knife, opened the blade, and went crawling over to the Mercedes. While the two in the Pontiac talked, covering the small scrapes and hissings he made, he slashed all four tires. It would be morning before they'd get this car running again.

As for the other one, the Pontiac, he couldn't hit the tires with those two guys in it, they'd feel the car shift. So he'd have to be more drastic. He crawled away behind a tree to get ready.

The bottle of gasoline, the strip of cotton cloth, the matches, when put together, became the revolutionist's delight, a home-made hand grenade, the weapon that used to be called the Molotov cocktail. Grofield lit it, stepped out from behind the tree, and tossed it.

The whole world lit up, red and yellow. There were two explosions, one after the other, as first the Molotov cocktail and then the Pontiac's gas tank went off. Bits of hysterical flame fell everywhere, and before the sound was out of the air Grofield was off and running.

He had maybe half a minute before they'd get over their surprise back there and start after him. In that time he could get well away from the fire glow, and then they'd play hell getting wind of him.

Grofield almost overshot the car, running along blind on the blacktop. But Elly had the window open and heard his footsteps, and whispered hoarsely, "Over here! Over here!"

He moved with arms stretched out in front of him, stumbled to the car, pulled the door open. The interior light went on, suddenly reassembling a chunk of space and reality, and he saw her face pale and frantic. "What did you do?"

"Gave us light. Let me behind the wheel."

She slid over and he got in. He started the engine, shut the door, but didn't turn on the lights. Ahead of him there was the flickering yellow-red glow. He drove toward it, more or less on the road.

The Pontiac was burning like a Yule log. In the dusty light, silhouettes of men ran around like cartoon characters, waving their arms. They saw the Datsun as it passed them and came running after it. The Mercedes was limping toward the road like a dachshund with broken legs.

"Down!" shouted Grofield. "Down!"

They drove by with their heads down, with Grofield's foot flat on the accelerator. They didn't hear the sound of the shots, but starred holes appeared in the windows, something thumped the door.

Then they were past, and Grofield switched on the headlights in time to see that the road meant to curve to the left. And start uphill.

"My God!" she said, staring back at the little dot of red. Then it was out of sight.

"Acapulco," Grofield said.

PART THREE

I

Acapulco. Friday morning, seven forty-five.

Governor Luke Harrison stepped from his cottage into the sunlight, gazed for a moment out at the blue blue sea, then strolled over and sat down at the table prepared for him beside his swimming pool. The water in the pool was also blue, but tinged with green. Two stewards began to serve breakfast.

The Governor was a tall man, heavyset, who through exercise and determination had kept himself in good physical condition through the years. He was the delight of his tailor, who did not for this one client have to strain his ingenuity to produce clothing that told white lies. His face was dominated by a strong, square jawline and by pale blue eyes of the utmost candor. His nose was perhaps a trifle too blunt, his mouth too thin-lipped, but all in all he successfully looked like what he was: a politician tending toward statesman, a former Governor, still an influential man in the upper circles of his party.

Influential, but not indispensable, not anymore.

Eating his breakfast, watching the sea, the Governor carefully kept his mind clear of all that, the past disappointments, the present dangers, the future uncertainties. Worry on first arising, worry during meals, worry at times of helplessness, all were bad for both the physical and mental well-being.

This place, the Hotel San Marcos, was an excellent distraction, lush and lovely to the eye, as breakfast was lush and lovely to the taste. It called itself a hotel, but was something other than a hotel, something more. The main building, downslope, was two stories

97

high, a rambling affair containing dining rooms, game rooms, offices, and so on. All the guests were in the smaller buildings scattered up the face of the steep hill behind that main structure, connected by gaily colored slate paths. There were square, two-story affairs containing four apartments, long, low bungalows of two apartments, and these single-occupancy cottages like the one where the Governor was staying and the one next door where Doctor Fitzgerald was still asleep.

All of these buildings had been carefully suited to the natural contours of the rocky hill, and built of stucco and painted pink. In front of each there was a small, pink-tiled swimming pool.

Down beside the main building were converted jeeps called sand buggies, with pink bodies and pink-and-blue striped tops. Each guest at the Hotel San Marcos had the free use of one of these sand buggies, which were seen bucketing around Acapulco all the time.

The town of Acapulco itself was built on a flat, curving stretch of beach in a fold of mountains. Mountains ringed it on three sides, a dramatic backdrop of dark green, with the pale blue tropical sky above and the darker blue of the Pacific stretching away flat to infinity on the remaining side, the south. This hill, at the eastern edge of town, afforded one of the best views to be had, and the Governor, as he ate, gazed out to sea with perfect pleasure.

The two stewards, one a Mexican born in Chilpancingo and the other an expatriate Guerreran who eight years ago had escaped from General Pozos' secret police, served the meal in deft silence. The Governor was unaware of their presence.

With the coffee and the cigar—the first of the day—that capped breakfast, he allowed the crowding worries to begin to attract his attention. There was Edgar, for one thing, and Edgar's idiot daughter, for another, and Juan, for a third, and young Bob, for a fourth, and his own plans for the future, for a fifth. Everything was so uncertain, so tentative, so complicated, so needlessly messy and sloppy.

Why didn't the old bastard just *die*, of his own accord, and be done with it? That would be simplest, taking everybody off the hook. No more worries about keeping Edgar keyed up to fighting pitch, no more fears that Ellen Marie would destroy everything, no more likelihood that Juan would turn his back on the Governor nor that Bob would—being so close, so close—guess the truth.

But it wasn't going to be simple and easy, because nothing in life ever is. Chomping on his cigar, glowering at the sea but no longer really seeing it, he mulled that thought, that nothing in life is easy and simple, no action is clearly and obviously good in all its ramifications nor bad in all its ramifications, that . . .

It was the girl, that was the main thing. Find her, hold her, *contain* her until this thing was done and over and forgotten, and all the other worries would fade into the background, would deflate to their proper size and importance. But the girl had to be found.

He'd been awakened at five this morning by a frantic phone call from Honner. The girl and that roustabout she'd picked up somewhere had broken through at Iguala, were on their way south now by road. It was two hundred and fifty miles, but all of it curving, twisting, narrow road through some of the wildest mountain country in the world; it was doubtful that they'd be able to make it in under seven hours, which would get them here no earlier than ten o'clock.

Not that they were likely to get this far. The Governor had told Honner to do what he should have done in the first place, call his other men here in Acapulco, have them start north as soon as it was light enough to travel. With Honner coming south, the others going north, they'd catch the girl in the middle, probably have her within an hour. They might even have her already, and not be near enough to a phone to report.

The thought pleased him. He was smiling as he looked to his right and saw Edgar Fitzgerald walking over from his cottage next door. The doctor looked haggard this morning, his suit rumpled on his big frame, his gray hair poorly brushed, but he said as he sat down in the other chair, "You don't have to study me that way, Luke. I'm all right today."

"Good. I never believed you wouldn't be. You want some coffee?"

"No. Any news?"

"Not a word. She probably isn't even in the country, Edgar. New York City is more likely, up there pouting and keeping to herself. She'll show up after this is all over."

The doctor shook his head. "She'll never forgive me, Luke, I know that. I've accustomed myself to the thought. She'll never understand, and she'll never forgive me." His brief smile was sour. "You give me bitter alternatives, Luke," he said. His eyes were red, as though he'd had too little sleep.

"We do what we have to do," the Governor told him. It was a sentence in an old argument, one he'd used half a dozen times in the course of persuading Edgar and keeping him persuaded. The sentence, by itself, now stood adequately in both their minds for the full argument.

The doctor nodded. "I know that. But it's hard, it's god-awful hard. I'll be glad when it's done, gladder than you'll ever know."

They were both widowers, the Governor for seven years and the doctor for three, and they had attained that shorthand of intimacy together that sometimes exists between widowers who have been friends for a long while. So the Governor did know what was going on in the doctor's mind, and he felt deep sorrow and honest remorse for being the cause of his friend's suffering. But he would do nothing to change it, nothing; he was stronger than his weaknesses.

He said, "When we're both at work, when this is in the past and we're *doing*, all these wounds will heal."

The doctor said nothing. He was gazing out to sea. When at last he did speak, what he said was, "Here they come."

The Governor looked, and here came General Pozos' yacht, all white and gleaming, turning slowly in at the harbor, beautiful and opulent and clean. A hard ball of undigested breakfast formed in the Governor's stomach. He heard a strange, strangled sound, and turned his head, and in the chair beside him Doctor Fitzgerald quite abruptly was crying.

2

GENERAL LUIS POZOS LAY asprawl in his bed between two women, with both of whom he was bored. In addition, he knew himself to be impotent this morning, which enraged him because it always frightened him when he was impotent, and this fear turned to rage was further turned to disgust, which he believed to be caused by the sleeping, round, warm, soft, musky bodies of the two women. They disgusted him, and he lay between them, on his back, their bodies pressing against him on both sides, and he worked his mouth beneath the thick black moustache, and raised his head, and spit in the face of the one on the right.

But it didn't wake her. The white ribbon drooled down across her cheek, down the line of her nose, down the faintly fuzzy flesh between nose and upper lip, and dripped at last, slowly, lazily, onto the gray and rumpled sheet.

He lowered his head again, weary now. Weary, and bored, and disgusted, and impatient. The room was too hot, the bodies pressed against him were too hot. He had a headache, and a stomachache. His left eye hurt. He was impotent. He had not slept enjoyably.

He raised his arms, brought his elbows together above his chest until they were nearly touching, then slashed sideways with the two elbows, each elbow striking a heavy breast, each elbow waking one of the disgusting women.

They awoke, and sat up in some confusion, the one on the left speaking rapid Spanish, the one on the right speaking staccato Dutch. Suddenly feeling more impatience and disgust and fury and boredom than he could stand, General Pozos began to flail about the bed with fists and knees and feet and elbows, kicking and punching and ramming until he'd knocked both of them out of bed and onto the floor.

Which struck him funny. All at once he flopped back down on the pillows, opened his mouth, and began to laugh. He had an odd, nasal, disquieting laugh, a kind of loud, hoarse coughing sound as though a buzzard were laughing. He lay on his back, holding his belly and laughing, while the two women got up from the floor and stood confused and chagrined, rubbing themselves where he had pummeled them. They looked at one another and at him and at the floor. They both felt humiliated and wanted to dress, but neither dared until the General let them know he had no more current use for them.

When his laughing fit was done, he found unexpectedly that he was in a pleasant mood. He scratched himself all over, with lazy hedonism, and asked the women to bring him his dressing gown. The Dutchwoman brought it over and gave it to him, and he heaved himself out of bed.

He was a short man, but big-boned, and would have been barrel-shaped no matter how he lived. His life being given over to relaxation and enjoyment and the sensual pleasures, this short, round frame had over the years been covered by layer after layer of heavy flesh, so that recently he had been described by an enemy—he had thousands—as "that beach ball with hair." His face showed the petulance of his nature, and he had softer, plumper hands than anyone else he had ever met, man or woman.

Once he was out of bed and into his dressing gown, it was proper for the two women to begin searching around the room for their own clothing. As they dressed, General Pozos spoke to them fondly, gently, telling them that today they were landing at Acapulco, a city in Mexico, a beautiful city of rich and happy people, a city in which he would be parting company with them. Yes, it was sad but true; their services were no longer required. Someone on the staff would see that they were taken care of, with money and documents of some sort, and that same someone would be delighted to answer whatever questions they might have on this or that topic. As for the General himself, he was saddened to be saying farewell to two such lovely and enchanting young ladies, but that of course is fate. Therefore—farewell.

Now, that is.

Both of them had been with the General long enough to know that he did all the talking, and that when he indicated a conversation was finished, it was advisable to quit his presence at once. They made the most perfunctory and brief of goodbyes, and left the room. They were both, in fact, relieved to be at the end of their relationship with General Pozos, both having heard the rumor—based on reality, as it happened—that the General one time, in a transitory rage of revulsion, had thrown one of his women off the yacht into the middle of the Pacific Ocean. Rescue operations had been instigated at once, naturally, but the unfortunate young woman had never been found. As she hadn't officially been aboard anyway, and as she'd additionally been traveling under an assumed name, there was never any trouble about the incident, nor any publicity, but rumors grow in the best-tended of gardens, the General's not excepted.

With the women gone, the General now rang for his dressers, two thin, silent, terrified young enlisted men in the Guerreran Army, whose salaries and training and maintenance were guaranteed by military aid from the United States. They dressed their General quickly but with great caution, and silently withdrew. The General was now in his uniform for the day, which he would wear until dinnertime, when he always changed into formal civilian clothes. Today's uniform was dark blue trimmed with gold. Fringed epaulets, a golden Sam Browne belt, an ornamental sword in a golden scabbard; he surveyed himself in a full-length mirror with great satisfaction. It gave him a pleasant feeling to wear a really good-looking uniform, and so he had over fifty of them, no two exactly alike. This dark blue was one of his particular favorites.

Wearing the uniform, buoyed up by his examination of it in the mirror, he left his stateroom at last and traversed the inner corridor to the dining room. Although he loved the sea, particularly from shipboard, he couldn't stand to look upon it before breakfast.

The dining room was empty except for young Harrison, sitting with a cup of coffee at one of the tables, reading a book. Quite a reader, this young man. Quite a studier, quite a silent type. It had occurred to General Pozos more than once to wonder what this young man from Pennsylvania actually thought of him, down inside; nothing ever showed on the surface, and that was unusual. With nearly everyone, the General could read their disposition toward him instantly in their faces, in their eyes—fear, or contempt, or envy, these were the most prevalent—but in the face, in the eyes of young Harrison, there was a bland nothing and less than nothing.

The General now came ponderously across the room, his scabbard ringing against a metal chair back, and sat down at the young man's table. "Good morning, Bob," he said, using the heavy, blunt English he took such pride in. "A lovely day," he added, because sunlight was pouring in the windows to his left.

Harrison looked up from his book, smiled promptly in that amiable, noncommittal way of his, and politely shut the book, not even marking his place. "Good morning, General," he said. "Yes, it is, one of the finest we've had this trip." He spoke fluent Spanish, but he knew the General preferred to speak English with him and so he obliged.

In nearly everything, in fact, Harrison was obliging and more than obliging. Only in one instance that the General could remember had Harrison refused to oblige, and then he had done so quietly, passionlessly, but permanently. That was the matter of the uniform. General Pozos preferred all members of his staff to be in uniform, though of course the uniforms must be plainer than his own, and this preference had gone unquestioned—as did his preferences generally—until he'd taken on young Harrison seven years ago. Harrison hadn't actually refused to be fitted for a uniform, but on the other hand, the fitting never took place. Whenever the General brought the subject up, Harrison broke immediately into an unending series of calm and sensible reasons why he should always be dressed in a business suit. He was more than willing to discuss the subject, would discuss it in his quiet and reasonable manner until the General couldn't stand the topic anymore, and would drop it as soon as the General made it clear he wanted to start talking about something else. These discussions were so tedious, so frustrating, and so unconquerable that the topic of Harrison's uniform gradually arose with less and less frequency and ultimately stopped arising altogether. Harrison never did get, or wear, a uniform, which was, so far as the General himself could remember, the only time in his career that his will had been successfully opposed.

Harrison now was wearing a gray linen suit in the narrow style, a dacron white shirt, and a pale gray tie. He was a well set-up young man, slightly over six feet tall, with a square, open, amiable, honest, typically American face, the sort of face ultimately typified by Colonel John Glenn. He wore his light brown hair in a casual crew cut, he occasionally donned horn-rim glasses when reading or working, and his fingernails were at all times scrupulously clean.

Observing him, reflecting on the fact that after seven years of close association he knew Harrison no better than when they'd first met, reflecting further on the undeniable truth that he trusted and relied on Harrison more than any other member of his staff—anyone else, yes, in the entire world—the General found himself sliding perilously close to uncomfortable thoughts and dangerous propositions. He cleared his throat noisily, clearing his mind at the same time, and said, "Well, you'll be pleased to see your father, I expect."

Harrison smiled. "Very much so, sir."

There was no way to tell if that were truth or politeness; everything Harrison did was so bland, so polite, so cooperative, so emotionless. *What does he think of me?* the General demanded in his head, and turned aside as the first steward approached with the grapefruit half that was his invariable first course at breakfast.

Conversation between them while the General ate was perfunctory and static; comments on the trip so far, on the coming meeting with Harrison's father, on the addition of Doctor Edgar Fitzgerald to the General's permanent staff. Harrison had more coffee, possibly because he wanted more coffee and possibly out of an accommodating desire to sit with the General while he ate.

The General's breakfast ended with coffee, hot and strong and black. The steward who served it was new, young, terrified, the ship rolled slightly, there was a second of imbalance, and the full cup of coffee was dumped in the General's lap.

The General acted without premeditation. Leaping away from the table in shock and pain, his right hand was already reaching out, closing around a fork, jabbing out, plunging the fork into the stomach of the petrified steward, who merely stood there ashen-faced and gaped. The fork tines were too short and too blunt to do any real damage, though they did break the skin. The fork fell to the floor, the steward staggered back a pace, and on his uniform there appeared four spreading dots of red.

What does he think of me? the General looked quickly at Harrison, to catch him unawares, while still startled by the accident and outburst.

Harrison was on his feet, bland, polite concern on his face as he extended his own napkin for the General's use.

3

JUAN POZOS SAT with *Time* magazine unread in his lap and looked out the window at the dark green of the mountains far below. Dawn glinted on the highest treetops down there, but the valleys were still deep in night.

The passenger sleeping in the seat beside him mumbled something in no language, shifted uncomfortably, and settled down again. Juan smiled ruefully at him, envying his unconscious state. The ability to sleep on airplanes he considered a mark of maturity, one of the many he had not as yet attained. He'd been airborne through the night this time, from Newark to New Orleans to Mexico City, and finally to Acapulco, and by now his eyes were burning from lack of sleep, but still they didn't want to close.

Not that there was any point in it now; they'd be landing in less than an hour. And wouldn't everyone be surprised to see him! Juan smiled in anticipation, seeing in his mind's eye the expression that would soon be on the face of Uncle Luke. Amazement, and delight. "How did you manage this, you young scamp?" "Got permission to skip my Friday classes." "Didn't miss anything important, I hope." (This said with an attempt at sternness that wouldn't fool a blind man.) "Oh, just a few tests," Juan would say, laughing, and Uncle Luke would laugh with him, put his arm around his shoulders, say, "Well, as long as you're here."

Juan smiled in anticipation. "Oh, just a few tests," he said in his mind. "Oh, just a few tests." The scene was as real as the mountains down there, as real as the thin black ribbon of road he could just glimpse here and there. Dawn sunlight semaphored from an automobile window.

The only problem was the General. If the General was drunk, or involved with women, or playing celebrity at some Hilton hotel, everything would be all right, the weekend could be very pleasant. But every once in a while the General decided to be a father, which meant he took a turn for the maudlin, slobbering on Juan's cheek, punching his whores in the face to demonstrate his moral reformation, and deciding Juan must come away from the USA, come back to Guerrero, come home and be a real son. "I'll buy you horses!" that was invariably the General's cry at such times. As though the addition of polo ponies would magically turn Guerrero into home.

Juan knew where home was. He'd just left it. That was why he was coming down now to talk with Uncle Luke.

So far as he was concerned, he would be physically present in Guerrero only once more in his life, and that would be on the occasion of the General's funeral. He didn't wish the General ill—was indifferent to his father's fate—but he knew that in the normal course of events the father precedes the son to the grave. His presence would be required for the funeral, and afterward he would probably have to go through some sort of formality in refusing to inherit his father's position. It might be best to have Uncle Luke along—assuming he was still alive at the time—to help Juan choose which man to support for the Guerreran presidency. It would be up to him to make that one contribution in directing his unhappy native land toward decent government, and then he could return to his own life, forgetting Guerrero forever.

That would please Uncle Luke, too. Juan knew that Uncle Luke wasn't happy about his impending graduation from college, and he knew it was because Uncle Luke was assuming he intended to go back to Guerrero once he had his hands on that BA. That was what Juan was coming to see Uncle Luke about now. Not only did he want to stay, but he wanted to go on with college.

It was all very clear in his head. He would borrow money from Uncle Luke—he'd already acknowledged the probability that the General would refuse to pay for any more schooling past the

BA—and he would insist on its being a real loan, not an outright gift. He was twenty-one now, and eager to begin taking on the responsibility of himself.

He'd thought it out with extreme care. For months he'd questioned himself about his plans for the future; did he really want to be an attorney, or was he choosing that career merely because he knew it would please Uncle Luke if Juan followed in his footsteps? But he was sure; the law was what he wanted, what he truly wanted.

United States law. Pennsylvania law.

It was unlikely, of course, that a Governor of Pennsylvania would ever be named anything like Juan Pozos, but it was not entirely beyond the realm of possibility. He had briefly considered changing his name to something more normal in his adopted country—perhaps even taking the last name of Harrison, or the first name of Luke, though not both—but he was too obviously Latin, with his olive complexion, glossy hair, smooth good looks. And it would be ignoble in any case to turn his back on his true origins. He considered himself an expatriate and an émigré, but not an escapee.

He was so completely the émigré, in fact, that Spanish now seemed to him a foreign tongue. He was, for this last leg of the trip from Mexico City to Acapulco, aboard an Aeronaves de Mexico plane, and when the stewardess had spoken to him in Spanish, he had at first failed to understand her, and then had blurted his answer in English. Then, when she responded in English, he made a belated switch to his rusty Spanish, creating the sort of awkward situation a twenty-one-year-old is seldom equipped to handle.

Incidents like that made him keenly aware of the anomaly of his position. He had lived most of his life in the States, but he was still a citizen of Guerrero. He thought of himself as an American and spoke most naturally in English, but his name and appearance were both clearly and permanently Latin. Uncle Luke, no blood relation to him at all, was by far the most important individual in his life, while his "real" father, whom he had been taught from childhood to call "General," was of importance only in a financial way, and even that would soon be coming to an end.

It seemed to him from time to time that a more delicate person might decide to be heavily neurotic and introspective and erratic in such a situation. As for himself, he had too much enjoyment of life to worry about abstract problems of identity. He enjoyed the University of Pennsylvania, he was delighted to have been taken under the wing of Uncle Luke, and he saw nothing in the foreseeable future to make him frown or worry or feel apprehension.

And there, out the window, under the wing, lay the royal blue of the sea. He had remembered to pack his bathing suit—the white one—and looking at the water far down there, he began uncontrollably to smile again.

The stewardess came around, waking the man beside Juan and telling him in Spanish that they were approaching Acapulco and he must put his seat belt on now. She looked at Juan, hesitated just an instant, and then told him the same thing in English. But she smiled, letting him know that she didn't think him merely a poseur, a fake gringo.

Juan clicked on his seat belt. "Oh, just a few tests," ran the joke line in his head, the scene clear and well rehearsed.

The plane circled interminably, giving him an endless series of views of the beauty of Acapulco; green mountains, blue sea, paler blue sky, white crescent of the town.

"Oh, just a few tests."

4

GOVERNOR HARRISON LOVED to drive the beach buggy, the converted jeep with its striped tin top. It was such a feckless, childish, irresponsible vehicle in appearance, and yet so rugged and reliable in performance. The perfect way to relax, to forget your troubles, to feel the weight of worry slip away and recapture the lost ebullience of youth.

After he'd calmed Edgar yet again, that grinding, painful, slow, unending task, the Governor had felt the need for therapy, for mindless relaxation, and so he'd come down the hill from his cottage, gotten into his candy-stripe buggy, and off he'd gone roaring into forgetfulness. Up over the mountain east of town and down the other side to El Marqués, in its own way a more exclusive and expensive resort than Acapulco next door. El Marqués, with its peculiar long beach of gray sand the color of coal ash, and the long, lazy breakers beating slowly upon it, with its few secluded old-style hotels and its occasional fenced-in private estates, was more than Acapulco the sort of place visited by politicians and heads of state. Dwight Eisenhower, in fact, had stayed at El Marqués one time while President of the United States. It was a mark of General Pozos' style and temperament that he should invariably choose the more public and obvious Acapulco.

Driving the beach buggy was fun, but there was no point arriving anywhere. This time Governor Harrison didn't even bother to drive as far as the beach, but turned around at the traffic circle by the naval base and drove back over the mountain again, passing the Hotel San Marcos and driving on into the town of Acapulco itself, past Hornos, the afternoon beach, all the way around to Caleta, the morning beach and dead end.

He got out of the buggy there a while and took off his shoes and socks and walked in the sand, leaving shoes and socks on the floor of the buggy. He walked this way and that, amid the bathers and the sunbathers. Boys tried to sell him straw hats and straw mats, serapes and wooden dolls, sandals and iced soda. If you were thirsty for alcohol you could have gin in a hollowed-out cocoanut with a straw. He wanted nothing.

From the beach he could see General Pozos' yacht, anchored out away from shore but within the harbor area. The launch had not yet left the yacht, and probably wouldn't much before noon.

Governor Harrison was surprised at how violently he didn't want to see General Pozos again. He felt contempt for the man, impatience, deep dislike, the same as ever, but these emotions no longer rode freely in his brain. The decision having been made, the plan now in operation, it seemed as though he were no longer free even to think poorly of General Pozos, as though the General were already dead and it would be bad form to harbor unkind thoughts about the dead.

Of course, there was Bob, too. How long had it been since he'd seen Bob? Seven, eight months, something like that. A man and his son drift apart when the son reaches his majority. Thinking about Bob, actually thinking about the boy for the first time in years, the Governor was surprised at the sudden realization that he no longer knew who Bob was. When had that happened, when had he lost contact with the boy?

God, years ago. When the son had been in his teens, the father was at his most active politically. And after that Bob had gone away to college, and now for the last seven years he'd been working for Pozos.

While Juan Pozos took his place.

Standing on the warm sand, feeling the sand between his toes and on the bottom of his bare feet, gazing out toward the yacht in the harbor all gleaming and white, Governor Harrison smiled crookedly and thought:

We've exchanged sons. While somehow he has become my enemy, and fate has decreed that I shall cause his death, he and I have exchanged sons. Why should General Luis Pozos be the man with whom my life is so entwined? Are we the two sides of the same coin, the two extreme examples of forms of government? Does God have a symbolic purpose in my causing the death of the dictator?

He was surprised to discover that he didn't want to see his son. In a way, he was afraid to see him.

That damn girl, he thought, *why don't they catch her?*

He turned away from the sea, walked heavily back through the sand to the beach buggy, and discovered that someone had stolen his shoes and socks. He looked around, glaring, and it seemed as though all the Mexicans nearby were looking at him sidelong and smirking. He had no doubt that every one of them had seen the robber, had seen the shoes and socks taken, and had done and would do nothing about it. The guilty one was probably still in plain view, sitting on the sand all smiling and innocent. With a sudden release for his foul mood, he swore angrily and climbed into the buggy and drove it violently back through town, cutting off other drivers and running a traffic light.

Back at the hotel, he stopped in at the main building to ask if there had been any phone calls, but there had not. Still barefoot, giving his anger free rein for the total relief of it, he strode up the path to his cottage to find Edgar still sitting there where the Governor had left him, smoking his pipe and gazing moodily out to sea.

The doctor saw him, and took the pipe from his mouth, saying, "Luke—"

"I don't have the patience for you now, Edgar. If it's more nonsense, I don't want to hear it."

The doctor said, in a tone of surprise, "What's happened to your shoes?"

The Governor opened his mouth to say something hasty and biting, but the sudden sound of the phone ringing in his cottage stopped him. "Later," he said, and hurried inside.

5

DOCTOR FITZGERALD SAT staring at the sea and pondered thoughts of death. Willful death. Murder, murder most foul.

No. Not murder *most* foul. In the case of General Pozos, it could well be murder *least* foul, the closest thing to truly justified homicide. But murder just the same.

Sitting in the sunlight while Luke was gone to answer the phone, Doctor Fitzgerald thought about what he was here to do, and wondered how he had come to such an intention. The stages of his conversion had been gradual and soft; he could be sure only that Luke Harrison, out of total conviction, had ultimately convinced him as well, and now the two of them were here to turn that conviction into action.

Of course, it was up to him actually to do the deed, but he neither blamed Luke for this nor considered it unjust. By his training and background, he was the only man for the job, it was as simple as that.

His one fear was that he wouldn't be able to last the ordeal. There would be no one there to talk to, no one to help him argue away his doubts. Luke daren't be anywhere near, and Luke's son was no part of the conspiracy. There were only the two of them in it; himself and Luke.

Well, no. Three now, including Ellen Marie. He had been foolish to talk to her, he realized that now, but he had desperately needed to talk to someone, and since Myra's death he had come to depend more and more on Ellen Marie for comradeship and understanding.

But this time she had understood nothing. He had tried to explain, but in his mouth Luke's arguments had sounded stiff and unnatural, and her first instinctive revulsion to the plan—hadn't that been his first reaction, too, long ago?—had never been overcome. And when at last they both had come to realize that neither could possibly alter the feelings of the other, she had made her wild threat to warn the General of what was to come.

Warn that tyrant, *warn* him! To do so would be to commit treason against the entire human race. Luke Harrison had said so and he himself had agreed. Could anyone possibly hold any sort of brief for General Pozos?

But nothing would change her mind, and so he had attempted to confine her, for her own good, until it all should be over, when he could attempt—with the deed finished and in the past—to reconstruct their shattered relationship. But she had gotten away, and where was she now? It was impossible even to guess. Luke had hired private detectives to try and find her, but so far they hadn't had any success at all. Apparently, if the private detectives were as good as Luke claimed they were, she hadn't come into Mexico at all, but was probably still somewhere in the States. Very possibly in New York or somewhere like that, sulking, as Luke maintained.

Of course, just in case she *was* in Mexico and still intended to try to talk with General Pozos, some of the private detectives were going to be here throughout the General's stay—only today and tonight, thank goodness—to keep her safely away, out of the General's sight and hearing.

The General. Doctor Fitzgerald thought of him again, and the plan again, and closed his eyes in torment. His pipe, long since out, hung slack from his mouth. He visualized the next days, weeks, months, as he would whittle away at the General's life.

Not that long, no, not that long. They had thought to make it last three months, an illness of three months' duration, but now that the time to begin was so close, the doctor realized he could never never never survive an ordeal like that for three long months.

Three weeks would be more like it, much more like it.

As he understood it, the current ocean voyage was scheduled to last another three weeks. That much he could probably survive, arranging it so that the General would sicken rapidly on the final stage of the trip, perhaps even to the point where it would have to be cut short. Yes, and have the General totally bedridden by the time they arrived finally at the palace in Santo Stefano. Then, in three or four more days, it could be finished.

He had just come to this decision, and was mulling it over, when Luke returned from his phone call.

Doctor Fitzgerald said, "Was that about Ellen Marie? Have they found her?"

"No, they haven't," said the Governor harshly. "I wish to Christ they would."

Doctor Fitzgerald turned his head, and here, coming up the tile path, suitcase in hand and broad smile on face, was the General's son, young Juan. In astonishment, forgetting everything else for the instant, the doctor exclaimed, "Well, look who's here!"

The Governor turned his head. Coming along past the swimming pool, beaming in obvious delight, Juan said, "Hi, Uncle Luke. How's everything?"

In the harshest voice the doctor had ever heard him use, the Governor snapped, "What the hell do you think you're doing?"

The doctor saw the smile collapse on Juan's face, saw the boy's expression become puzzled and hurt, and all at once he thought: *It's his father we're going to kill*. And he saw why he had been foolish to tell Ellen Marie, to expect her to make the kind of dispassionate moral judgment necessary to understand what it was he had to do.

Juan, stumbling, bewildered, embarrassed, was saying, "I just, I just flew down to see you."

"Well, you can turn right around," the Governor said, in the same cold, harsh voice, "and just fly right back again." Spinning on his heel, the Governor stalked into his cottage and slammed the door behind him.

Juan had dropped his suitcase, and now he turned to the doctor, spreading his hands in a helpless gesture, saying, "I was only, only . . ."

THE CALL had been from Honner, telling the Governor that Ellen Marie Fitzgerald and the man with her were dead.

Life had been hectic for Honner since three o'clock this morning, when all at once the Pontiac had blown up and the Mercedes had turned out to have four slashed tires. The girl and the son of a bitch with her had gone tearing on by, in the clear, and that was that.

Honner was the first of the survivors to get over his excitement and panic. The others wanted either to start running down the highway after the Datsun's taillights or throwing dirt on the burning Pontiac. Neither move made any sense, since you couldn't catch a Datsun on foot and there was no percentage in trying to put the fire out. The two guys in the Pontiac were dead already, so let them cook.

Honner got the rest organized again. That's what he was for, that's what his reputation was all about. He got the other three rounded up, and they all packed themselves into the Mercedes and drove into Iguala on the rims.

Iguala was asleep, so asleep it was nearly dead. Honner finally found a telephone and called another of the Governor's men in Mexico City. The Mercedes was still the best car for the job down here, better than anything else they might come up with at this time of night, so Honner told the man in Mexico City to get hold of four new tires and send them down with somebody to put them on the car. Honner considered calling Governor Harrison then, too, but it was a hell of an hour at night and there wasn't anything to report by way of success, so he decided to wait till later.

At five o'clock, even though the new tires hadn't arrived and he couldn't yet start out on the trail again, Honner felt he could no longer delay giving the Governor the news. So he called, and told the Governor what had happened, and the Governor told him to call Borden, one of his men in Acapulco, and tell him to start north, watching for the girl. They'd catch her in a pincers.

Fine. That sounded good, and it sounded sure, and that made Honner a lot happier. And when the new tires came, shortly after five-thirty, already on rims and set to be slapped on the car, Honner was happier yet. He picked one man, Kolb, to go with him, told the others to follow along in the Chevrolet that had brought the tires down, and headed south at top speed.

He left the Chevrolet out of sight behind him before he reached the really bad road. For most of its southern half, the Mexico City–Acapulco highway is a road far more scenic than navigable. It travels through green mountains, twisting and turning, climbing and descending through some of the wildest, emptiest, most beautiful and terrifying scenery in the world. Hairpin curves are constant as the road pokes its way up and down the cliff faces. On every side are the dark green mountains, slashed here and there with raw rock where the road has been blasted through, so that when climbing toward a high pass it is possible to look out over a cliff drop of hundreds of feet, to look down through clouds drifting past the slopes below you, and see *there* a bit of road you traversed ten minutes ago and over *there* another section you won't be reaching for ten minutes more.

To make any speed at all on a road like this was impossible, so here the great advantages of the Mercedes over the Datsun were minimized, though the Mercedes could still handle the curves at somewhat better speeds. Honner drove hard, and well, and averaged nearly forty miles an hour.,

Until, at ten minutes past nine, rounding a particularly sharp curve high in the mountains some ninety miles north of Acapulco, Honner very nearly crashed into a white Ford coming the other way. Both drivers slammed on the brakes and the cars shivered to a stop next to one another, where the drivers stared at one another blank-faced.

The other driver was Borden, the Governor's man from Acapulco.

Honner and Borden got out of their cars and faced one another in the middle of the road. Honner said, "You let them through, you moron, they're in a white Datsun."

"They didn't pass me, brother, I'll swear to it," said Borden. "I saw two vehicles the whole time since I left the city, one of them a blue Karmann Ghia with two bearded guys in it and no room for anybody else, and the other an oil truck with a guy alone in the cab, which I know for sure because I stopped him and asked directions."

Honner frowned and looked off the other way. One car had passed him since Iguala, headed north, and that had been an old Citroën with a family aboard, the back seat full of kids. Besides, there was no point in the girl turning around and going north again.

Honner said, "Then they got off the road somewhere and let you go by, and took off again behind you."

"No, sir. I thought they might try something like that, and I was ready for it. They hid no place, I'll say that for a fact. You know yourself what this road is like. Most places there's barely enough space for two cars *on* the road, much less off it."

"Still and all," said Honner, "that's got to be what happened. Turn around, we'll check it out."

"And you'll see I'm right."

They both headed south then, watching both sides of the road, and it was true there were no turnoffs, no lanes, no places to move a car into and hide it from anyone on the road.

Abruptly Honner pulled to a stop, at a place where the road came to a peak, angled sharply to the left, and dropped downhill again. Here was one of the few places where a gravel widening had been constructed beside the road where people could stop to rest and look at the view. A single-rail, rustic log fence ran along the edge of the cliff here, and one of the log rails was missing.

Honner walked over to look, and to his unpracticed eye it seemed as though faint tire tracks led out to the edge and over. Kolb and Borden and the two men with Borden all squinted at the ground, too, and agreed with him it did look that way. Tire tracks, and scrape marks at the edge.

Honner disliked heights. He lay down on his stomach and inched toward the edge until his head was peeking over. He held his breath, worried about vomiting, and looked down.

It was nearly a straight drop, and it looked like forever. There were trees in clusters down the cliff face, and a sea of dark green trees at the bottom. Looking, staring, squinting, Honner finally made out the path of something, saw where tree branches had been sheared away here and there, saw the faint evidences of a straight line leading down, and down, and down . . . to a trace of whitish color at the very bottom. Yes, there it was, so small and so far away he'd very nearly missed it. But it was there, it was definitely there.

Honner crawled away from the edge. He felt relief at not looking over there anymore, but nothing in particular about either the girl nor the man with her. He didn't harbor grudges nor think of vengeances.

He got to his feet and said, "Let's get to a phone."

7

THE GOVERNOR WANTED to make it up to the boy. No, he didn't truly want to, but he had to. With everything else crowding in on him, he had to stop everything and nursemaid the stricken Juan.

He could feel the falseness of his smile stretching his cheeks as he came out by the pool, flopped with an attempt at casualness onto a chaise near the boy, and said, "Well, that's better! Good to see you, boy!"

Juan's own smile was uncertain as he said, "It was supposed to be a surprise."

"It was that, all right! Eh, Edgar?"

The doctor smiled nervously. "Yes, indeed."

Juan said, "I'm sorry if I did anything—"

"No no no! I'm always glad to see you, Juan, you know that. If you managed to wangle a day or two away from the grind, more power to you, say I! Just ignore the way I acted, you know how I am in the morning sometimes."

"Uncle Edgar said you'd gotten a phone call that upset you."

"He did?" The Governor, startled, looked past Juan at the doctor. The man couldn't possibly know about Ellen Marie's death, there was no way for him to know it. And he wouldn't just sit there, weak and nervous, his usual pallid self.

The doctor said, "I told Juan that was probably why you snapped at him. I hope it wasn't anything serious."

"Oh, no," said the Governor, understanding now but too harried to be grateful for Edgar's quick thinking. "Nothing serious, just a mix-up about the dinner party. Yes, and we'll have to find a place for you, too," he told the boy. "Near your father, if we can manage it."

"Don't go to any special trouble for me," Juan said.

"Nonsense, boy."

The doctor said, "I suppose you're looking forward to seeing your father again, eh?"

"I suppose so," said Juan, unconvincingly.

The Governor said, "After graduation, he'll see him all the time. Isn't that right, Juan?"

"No, sir," said Juan.

They both looked at the boy in surprise, the Governor feeling a sudden tightening in his stomach. Something else? Would nothing hold still for a man? He said, unable to keep the ragged edge out of his voice, "No? What do you mean, no? You'll be going home."

"Uncle Luke, I—" The boy hesitated, glanced at Edgar, and started again, "Home is Pennsylvania," he said. "The United States. I don't know Guerrero, I don't have any feelings about it, on the plane when the stewardess—Uncle Luke I—I want to stay with you."

It was the doctor who said it: "But, your father."

The boy turned, and it was obviously much easier for him to speak through the doctor rather than directly. "He isn't really my father," he said. "We don't even know each other, we don't really want to know each other. Uncle Luke is the one I know, the one I'm— I feel like a member of *his* family, not some, some banana-republic General I don't even know." He turned back to the Governor, straining with the urgency to be understood. "I'm an American, Uncle Luke," he said. "Not a Guerreran. I haven't been that since I was a little kid. I want to stay. I want to study law."

Through his growing frustration, the Governor was still conscious of the honor Juan was doing him, but he pushed the awareness away; it led to layers of moral complexity, of conflicting loyalties and a confusing welter of choices, none entirely good. Spreading his hands, he said, "I don't know what to say."

The doctor said, "Juan, there are people, I mean people in your own country, in Guerrero, they're depending on you."

"No one even knows me there."

"Oh, no, that's where you're wrong. Your father—I don't know if you knew this, but he isn't at all well. He could go any time, and there are people, people down there in Guerrero, they're depending on you to take over, to uh, to lead your people, to, well—"

"To be a puppet on strings," Juan said fiercely. "I know all about that, what they want. The same crowd running things, with me standing on a balcony two or three times a year. But that isn't what I want, that hasn't anything to do with me, who I *am*." Turning back to the Governor, he said, "You understand, Uncle Luke, don't you? I've got to be where I feel I belong."

This was dangerous, and entirely unexpected. The Governor wet his lips. "'Well, it depends," he said carefully, "on what you want, of course, on the life you want for yourself. But there are other things, too, things to be taken into account. You can't just thrust power away, you know, not if it's in your hands. Power brings responsibility, Juan."

"Oh, I'd try to turn the government over to the best people I could find," the boy said. "But that's in the future, that isn't the point. The point is I want to go on with my schooling, I want to become an American citizen. All this other stuff . . . When the General dies, we can talk about it then. You could even help me, go down there with me, help me pick the best men to take over."

"I suppose I could," said the Governor thoughtfully, seeing where it all might yet work out. Maybe even better, without Juan. Choose the people who would fit in best with his own plans, have Juan give them his support, then ship Juan back to the States. Have the government "run" by men with straightforward political debts to himself, that would be much simpler in the long run than having to clear everything through a naïve and inexperienced boy. "You might be right," the Governor said. "And frankly, I hadn't been looking forward to losing you after graduation."

"You won't lose me, Uncle Luke," Juan said. "You couldn't possibly lose me."

Looking past the boy's shining face, the Governor saw Edgar gazing at the boy with an expression of such wistfulness that he could only be thinking of his daughter, wondering where she was, how to end the rift between them.

For the first time, the Governor saw how close he was to losing everybody, absolutely everybody. This plan was bringing him to the brink, everything was riding on it. And the balance was so delicate, so delicate; one injudicious push in any direction could throw the whole thing off, lead to exposure, ruin, failure.

Edgar must not know about Ellen Marie's death, not until afterward. It had been an accident, but even so. At this juncture, it would be fatal for Edgar to learn what had happened.

There were too many things to think about, too many things to guard against. All he could do now was push forward, forward. Try to keep all the strings in his hands. Try to keep on top of the situation.

Smiling with forced briskness, he said, "Enough of this now. Is this a vacation or what is it? Juan, let's us go for a swim."

THERE WAS a time when Richio had been considered handsome, but that was in the days before his stay at the Malenesta Prison, in the days before he lost his left eye and collected the raised road map of scars crisscrossing his body from forehead to knee. No one considered Richio handsome these days; no one considered him anything but terrifying.

Lerin was frankly afraid of Richio, though he himself had been confined briefly at the same prison and knew firsthand something of the life Richio had lived. But few men had gone through as much as Richio and survived at all; it was too much to hope that a man would go through all that and survive sweet-tempered. A murderous rage lived inside Richio, just beneath the skin; it never slept, and almost anything could call it forth.

On the other hand, Lerin had no desire to lose his job, and if he delayed much longer, he would be late returning to the hotel. The Hotel San Marcos did not tolerate laxness or tardiness in its staff. Lerin had come up the hill to the poor section of Acapulco, the native, non-tourist section, and just outside Richio's room he'd been told by Maria that Richio was still asleep, Richio had drunk far too much last night, Richio was snorting with rage in his sleep and would surely awake as surly as a donkey, as vicious as a snake.

Richio's room was directly off the dirt street, through a slanting wooden door in the long white wall and into a dark, dirt-floored, evil-smelling room seven feet square. In here Richio slept away his hangovers, his bad dreams, his evil frustrations, coming out usually only after sundown to cadge and steal his way through the evening, drink his way through the night. Sometimes he lived alone, sometimes he shared his life with a woman; currently, with Maria, a squat whore from one of the border cities, brought here by a Texan in an air-conditioned Pontiac, left behind like a toothbrush. No one knew what Maria thought of Richio; no one cared.

Lerin had paced back and forth in the dusty street for a quarter of an hour now, watched by the phlegmatic Maria as she squatted in the thin shade of the building. From time to time he heard the snorting and thrashing of Richio in there, and once Richio called out, hoarsely, perhaps calling for help, perhaps only calling down curses on the phantoms that oppressed him.

Lerin stopped his pacing. "He must be waked," he said. "There is no help for it."

Maria shrugged.

"If I wake him, he will be angry," Lerin said, talking more to himself than the girl. "If I don't tell him now, and the boy goes away again this afternoon, he will be more angry."

Maria shrugged.

"So I wake him," said Lerin, trying to convince himself of his decisiveness. Taking a deep breath, he moved forward, pushed ajar the door, and stepped into Richio's room.

The room smelled like the breath from Richio's open mouth; gaseous, rotting, humid. There was a bed along the rear wall, made of wood, covered with faded blankets that had once been bright-colored. A chair on the left was the only other furniture.

Richio was sprawled naked across the bed on his stomach, an arm and a leg hanging over the side. His face was turned toward Lerin, his mouth was hanging open to show his few teeth. His good right eye was out of sight against the blanket, leaving only the shriveled socket of the left showing, like an inverted red prune. He was fearfully ugly, and vicious, and violent, and Lerin approached him with dry mouth and nervous hands.

"Richio," he said softly, almost whispering, and the man on the bed snarled in his sleep, moved his arms vaguely, settled down again. "Richio. Richio."

Nothing more. Lerin moved reluctantly closer, reached out, touched Richio on the shoulder.

Richio came roaring off the bed, hands like claws. Jumping back, Lerin stumbled over his own feet, fell heavily to the dirt floor. Richio was on him like a cat, straddling him, closing his hands around Lerin's throat. Richio's face blazed with madness.

"Richio! Richio! Richio!" Lerin screamed the name over and over, trying to bring Richio to his senses before the hands cut off his wind, and all at once the struggle stopped, Richio's hands dropped away, Richio sat on Lerin's stomach and said, "What the hell you doing?"

"I had to talk to you."

Richio casually smacked him openhanded across the face, partly in friendly humor and partly in continuing irritation. "You want to talk to me. What would a moron like you have to say to a moron like me?"

"His son is here. In Acapulco."

Richio leaned forward, his heavy face directly above Lerin's. "The son? You've seen him?"

"He just came to the hotel."

"And Pozos? Not with him?"

"No, he's with two gringos. Older men. They speak English and he calls them 'uncle.'"

Richio got to his feet, rubbing his hand against his face. "To meet his father? Why come here? You meet your old man at home, not someplace else."

"The other men didn't expect him. I heard them talk a little, and he came as a surprise."

"Surprise." Richio nodded. "We'll give him a surprise." He went to the doorway, said to Maria, "Get me some water," Standing there, he urinated in the street.

Lerin said, "I have to get back soon."

"They watch Pozos," Richio said. "A man can't get near the bastard. But not the son, eh? How would he like that, the bastard? Cut down his only son, eh? Would he feel *that*, the bastard?"

"I have to get back, I don't want to lose my job."

"That will do just as well," Richio said. "Let Pozos live. Let him live without a son."

Lerin said, "One thing, please. Don't do it when I'm around."

Richio looked at him in heavy surprise. "I'll do it when the chance is good," he said. "You just be sure you aren't there."

Now that he'd told, Lerin was beginning to regret it. But the other way would have been just as bad; if he hadn't told Richio, and afterward Richio found out the son had been at the hotel, Richio would kill *him* as a handy substitute.

Maria brought in a metal pail half full of water. Taking it from her, Richio raised it to his lips, filled his mouth, gargled, spat on the floor. Then he drank, for a long while, and finally poured the remainder of the water over his head, wetting his body and more of the floor.

"I have to get back," Lerin said.

Richio took a blanket from the bed, began to use it to rub himself dry. "I'll see you later," he said.

THERE WERE TIMES when Juan took a somewhat guilty pleasure
in the fact of his own beauty. He *was* beautiful, in an entirely
masculine way, straight and lean of body, clear of eye, with
unlined brow and gleaming smile, but most of the time he remained unself-conscious about himself, not thinking about his
appearance at all beyond the simple level of striving for neatness
and cleanliness. But there were moments when the fact of his
beauty was so forcefully present that he himself became aware of
it, and at such moments he was delighted by himself, all the while
feeling it was somehow wrong to take such pleasure—almost
girlish pleasure—in the accident of one's looks.

Now, dressed in his white bathing trunks, poised at the edge of
the small swimming pool, was one of those moments. He knew
the contrast of white trunks and olive skin was pleasing to the
eye, knew his physique was good, his face handsome, his movements virile and graceful. He could see it reflected in the eyes of
Uncle Luke, already treading water in the pool, and Uncle
Edgar, sitting in a lounge chair on the other side of the pool.

When he found himself delaying his dive into the water,
posing at the brink like some movie queen, his self-consciousness
turned into embarrassment and he dove awkwardly into the
water, coming up sputtering to hear Uncle Luke's hearty laugh-
ter.

"Was that a belly-whopper! How'd you get to be so graceful?"

"Practice," Juan said, the embarrassment gone as quickly as it had come. He floated on his back, closing his eyes against the high late-morning sun. For a while he just floated and relaxed and lazily thought his thoughts behind closed eyes.

Mostly that nothing ever works the way you think it will, not exactly. Like the scene he'd planned for meeting Uncle Luke, blown up by the coincidence of Uncle Luke's being mad about a phone call just at the wrong time. And his plan to talk to Uncle Luke calmly, quietly, perhaps over dinner, instead of which he'd blurted it out right away, with no preparation, nothing organized in his head.

That was mostly because of the awkwardness of the meeting. He had strongly felt that Uncle Luke needed something to cheer him up, something to take his mind off his irritation and the strained atmosphere between them. It was as though he had wanted to present Uncle Luke with some sort of gift, and the only gift he had was himself, his continuing to live in the United States, his total conversion to his adopted country.

And then even that had gone unexpectedly, with Uncle Luke at first seeming to disapprove. Uncle Edgar, too, even more so. But Juan thought he understood that now, at least Uncle Luke's objection. He'd been bending over backward to be fair, that's all, serving as a kind of devil's advocate for himself, wanting to be sure Juan wasn't making a spur-of-the-moment decision he'd regret later on.

But everything was all right now. They hadn't discussed the finances yet, but there was no hurry about that. Juan already knew how it would go; at first Uncle Luke would insist on paying for everything himself, making a gift of it, but as Juan would persist, Uncle Luke would finally accept the fact that it was a loan.

There was no hurry, though. That conversation could wait a week or a month or even more. He would give it better timing than the first half. Patience, like sleeping in airplanes, was a mark of maturity, and it was about time he started developing some of those marks.

"Juan!"

He opened his eyes, rolled lazily in the water. Uncle Luke was standing up by the side of the pool, grinning down at him. Juan called, "What's up?"

"Going to give you a diving lesson," Uncle Luke said. "Watch carefully, now. See how it's done."

Juan, treading water, watched Uncle Luke with fond pleasure. If he could look half that good at Uncle Luke's age he'd be well pleased. There was a man who kept himself in top condition both physically and mentally, and Juan, looking up at him, realized just how lucky he was to have been brought up by such a man. "Okay, Tarzan," he called. "Show me."

Uncle Luke sliced into the water with hardly a ripple, curved to the bottom and up like a long, sleek tan fish, broke the surface with a shout of pleasure and turned to call, "*That's* how it's done!"

"Oh, you go in on your stomach. I didn't know that."

Uncle Luke snorted. "Stomach my foot!"

Juan, laughing, recited, "You are old, Father William—"

"Be off," shouted Uncle Luke, "or I'll throw you downstairs!"

"I'll show you a dive," Juan promised, and glided to the edge of the pool. He lifted himself up out of the water, stood on the pink cement, and shook water out of his ears.

"This way to the Olympics!" called Uncle Luke.

Juan stood at stiff attention by the edge, hands at his sides. "Ze vay ve dife in Chermany," he said, "is shtraight up und den shtraight down."

"Like a stone," commented Uncle Luke, and across the pool Uncle Edgar was smiling at them both.

Juan changed his stance, making his body loose and sinuous. "In India," he said, "we dive like a ssssssnake, rrrrrippling srough se water."

"In Mexico," Uncle Luke called, "we mostly stand beside the pool and talk big."

"There are times—"

Uncle Edgar shouted, "Look out!"

Juan saw Uncle Edgar half out of his chair, staring at something behind Juan, his face distorted by shock. Juan turned to see what it was, and couldn't believe his eyes.

Running toward him was a half-naked man dressed only in dirty khaki pants. He was the ugliest man Juan had ever seen, his body ridged and corroded by scars. He was running downhill over the boulders, far from any of the slate paths, and held rigid in his right hand was a gleaming knife.

10

DOCTOR FITZGERALD couldn't move.

He was half-in, half-out of his chair, most of his weight supported by his arms, his hands clutching the chair arms. Suspended that way, as though time had frozen with him in the process of getting to his feet, he watched the drama on the other side of the swimming pool.

The man with the knife had apparently circled most of the hotel buildings in order to come down from above, and had managed to come very close without being observed, actually running across the open only in the last ten yards or so. He seemed unaware of the existence of anyone but Juan, rushing straight at him, ignoring the doctor's shouts or the shouts of Luke Harrison, still down there in the pool.

Luke, too, was frozen, standing chest-deep in the water near the shallow end, one arm raised up out of the water in a half-completed gesture, as though he'd been about to ask the others to give him their attention. Like Edgar, he watched, without moving, the contest between Juan and the man with the knife.

The contest. Juan had had just enough warning to evade that first headlong rush, jumping to one side, leaping over a lounge chair and then kicking the chair into the other man's path.

The whole thing had almost turned farcical at that point, when for just an instant the assailant teetered off balance and it seemed as though his only choice lay between falling over the lounge chair or tumbling into the pool. His arms flailed, the knife glinted in helpless malevolence in the sunlight, and then the instant was gone, he had his balance again, and he was turning to find Juan once more and finish the job he'd started.

Juan had backed away, but for some reason he didn't turn and run. Instead he stood there, perhaps ten feet from the other man, watching and waiting, poised like a cat. Doctor Fitzgerald heard him say, "What's the matter? I don't know you."

The other man moved forward, half-crouching, the knife held out to one side. He weaved back and forth as he came on, almost as though trying to hypnotize Juan, and Juan watched him as closely as a child watching a magician, trying to see by what trickery the rabbit is being made to come out of the hat.

The distance between them narrowed, to eight feet, six feet, and again the other man leaped forward. Again Juan jumped backward, this time almost falling over a lounge chair himself, but getting his balance back, grabbing a white towel off the seat of the chair, dancing away out of range of the knife.

Juan spoke again, this time in Spanish. The other one, standing by the chair that Juan hadn't quite tripped over, rested his free hand on the chair back, as though this were a brief time-out they were taking, and answered in harsh, guttural Spanish, spitting the words out. Juan's face twisted, in pity or disgust, and the time-out was over.

The man went to his left around the chair, and Juan went the other way, circling the chair. The man, with an angry shout, kicked the chair out of the way. Juan ran nimbly past him, and now they were moving in the opposite direction, back toward where they had started.

There was a terrible fascination in watching the two of them, so violently contrasted, the boy so fresh, smooth, handsome, the other so twisted and scarred. Both moved with fine grace, the boy light as a deer, the man with the heavy grace of a panther.

Whatever the man had said, Juan seemed slowed now, just slightly unsure of himself. As though in some strange way he found merit in the other's case, a justification for murder that he could not himself entirely rebut. He seemed not to be looking for a way to escape, nor for a way to beat the other, but for an answer, as though somewhere in his head he had to find words to use against the knife.

Why doesn't he run? the doctor asked himself. Why doesn't Luke do something, say something? It didn't occur to him to wonder at his own silence; he knew he could neither move nor speak, and he accepted the knowledge without question.

Over on the other side of the pool, it was like a dance, like modern ballet. Juan moved only when the other man did, and only enough to keep clear of the knife. As for the other one, his movements had grown smaller, more controlled, as though he was afraid of lunging too carelessly, losing his advantage. Or perhaps he was simply like the cat with the mouse, prolonging the chase for his own pleasure, though his expression seemed too grim and humorless and intent for that.

"Juan!"

It was Luke, finally coming out of it, calling from the water. Juan half-turned his head when his name was called, the man with the knife darted forward, Juan jumped back. He flicked the towel at the man's face, but missed.

Luke shouted, "Get away from him, Juan! Run down the hill! Run down the hill!"

The man seemed to think Juan would do as Luke wanted; in any case, he all at once rushed forward, flailing with the knife. Juan, running backward, flicked the towel again, this time at the knife, once, twice—and the knife went flashing through the air, spun away by the towel. It fell clear of the tile, landed point down in the earth, the handle quivering there.

The man stood flatfooted an instant in astonishment, gaping at his empty hand. Then, with a roar of humiliation and rage, he rushed Juan bare-handed, his fingers reaching out for Juan's throat.

Juan caught him by the wrists, and they staggered back and forth, clamped together, hands to wrists, the muscles straining in their arms and across their shoulders. Even their bellies were tight and rippled with the strain, and on Juan's bare legs the thigh muscles were bunched and knotted. They bent this way, that way, both showing their teeth in wide grimaces, their eyes unblinking as they stared at one another.

Until with a sudden movement the other man twisted free, stumbled back, and rushed forward again. This time Juan sidestepped him, grabbing him by the upper arm, using his own movement against him, pushing him around in a floundering half-circle. Juan's foot came out, the other tripped, hit the tile hard on his left shoulder, and rolled despairingly over the edge into the pool.

Luke was on him like a bull, holding him down, pressing him, mashing him down into the water.

Doctor Fitzgerald, released from tension, sank back into the chair. He inhaled, a long, shuddering, painful breath that seared the inside of his chest, making him wonder how long it had been since he'd breathed. "Thank God!" he whispered. Shooting pains were running up and down his arms; he let them dangle over the sides of the chair, and gave himself over to catching his breath.

Across the way, Juan had fallen to the tile, was sitting there spraddle-legged like a rag doll, like a puppet whose strings have been cut. And in the pool Luke was hulked in chest-deep water, grim and intent, holding, holding. Beneath him the water thrashed in violence.

Slowly Juan seemed to come aware of the world again, and then of Luke and of what was happening. His face twisted with pain, Juan leaned toward the pool, calling, "Uncle Luke, don't!"

But Luke paid no attention to the boy, and beneath him the agitation in the water was lessening.

Juan slid forward to hands and knees, crawled to the edge of the pool, cried, "Uncle *Luke!* Stop it!"

Doctor Fitzgerald, watching and listening, finally roused himself, sat up, and called, "Let him go, boy. He knows what he's doing, let him go." And then realized, in some astonishment, that he'd only whispered, that no one could have heard him, and that he hadn't really expected to be heard.

Juan, his exhaustion showing in every movement, lumbered clumsily into the pool, falling more than diving, and struggled over to Luke. Then a strange silent struggle went on, the two fighting like tired sharks for the thing in the water. Luke muttered something that Doctor Fitzgerald couldn't hear, and to which the boy made no answer, then all at once turned his back, leaving it all to Juan. Luke came slowly over to this side of the pool, arms held up out of the water, and stopped with his forearms resting on the tile. He looked up at the doctor with expressionless eyes and said, "Call the police, Edgar." His voice was quiet, calm.

Across the way, Juan was dragging the man—unconscious, or dead—out of the water. The doctor said, "Of course," and got to his feet. His entire body was stiff, the nerves jumping, as though he'd been beaten all over with blackjacks. Shaking, his body unaware that it was all over, he hobbled toward the cottage to make the call.

11

GOVERNOR HARRISON SAT panting in a deck chair and watched Juan, across the pool, giving the son of a bitch artificial respiration. He wanted to tell the boy to quit it, let the son of a bitch die, but he didn't have the strength to raise his voice, and when all was said and done, it really didn't matter.

Juan was still alive.

While it was going on, the Governor had been too frozen with horror to do anything but watch that goddamn moron try to stick a knife into everything he'd been working for. Now that it was over, his anger at the failed assassin was mostly reflexive; he was feeling too much relief at Juan's being alive to have much emotion to spare for imbeciles.

And what could the man be but an imbecile? In broad daylight, he comes running out of nowhere, barefoot, naked to the waist, ugly as sin, brandishing a knife, trying to murder a perfect stranger right in front of two witnesses.

An escapee from an insane asylum, more than likely. A candidate for an asylum, at any rate.

Across the way, Juan was straddling the lunatic, pumping away at his back, just as though it were important that maniacs go on breathing. But if it made the boy feel any better, let him go to it.

Edgar came back out of the cottage, walking like a man with broken kneecaps. His face was as white as wax. He said, "They're sending for the police. And two men will come up to hold him till the police get here."

"Good."

From across the pool, Juan called, "Uncle Edgar! Will you take a look?"

"Oh," said Edgar, like a sleepwalker. "Of course."

The Governor watched him walk around the pool, legs as shaky as a foal's, and he found it impossible to believe that such a man would be able to accomplish what must be done. How to put steel in that back?

If only Pozos were responsible for Ellen Marie's death. Of course, in a way he was; if it hadn't been for the existence of Pozos, Ellen Marie would still be alive, but that was reasoning of too subtle a sort to try on a man just bereft of a daughter.

Was there any way? Somehow make Pozos to blame, that would do the trick. Edgar would perform like a machine, absolutely without emotion, given such an emotional reason.

Juan was coming around the pool now, leaving Edgar on his knees beside the lunatic. Juan smiled shakily and dropped into the chaise beside the Governor, saying, "Uncle Edgar says he's all right."

"Tomorrow I'll be glad," the Governor said. "Right now I'm sorry I didn't do the whole job."

Juan reached out and pressed his hand on the Governor's knee. "I appreciate that, Uncle Luke," he said, "I appreciate what it means you feel about me, but you don't understand about that man."

"Understand what? He's a lunatic, that's all."

"He was in one of my father's prisons. That's where he got all those scars."

The Governor glanced across the pool, then back at Juan. "Is that what he told you?"

"Yes, sir."

"Why try to kill you? Why not go after your father?" And save me, the Governor thought, all this trouble.

Juan shrugged. "I don't know. I suppose my father's too well guarded. And I guess he thought this would be a good revenge, kill the General's only son." Juan laughed without humor, "If he only knew."

"Knew what?"

"I'm hardly General Pozos' son," Juan said. "You know that. He doesn't care about me and I can't bring myself to care about him."

Two men came up then, employees of the hotel. The Governor gestured across the pool, saying, "Over there, that's him."

The assassin—attempted assassin, thank God—was sitting up now, groggily. Edgar had been speaking to him, softly, but now he straightened and backed away as the two hotel employees came over. They stood uneasily on either side of the sitting man, looking at him or at the pool or at each other, obviously not entirely sure what was called for from them in such a situation.

Edgar came around the pool and sat down in the chaise on the Governor's other side. "He'll be all right," he said. "He swallowed some water, but Juan got most of it up."

"I almost want to let him go," said Juan. When Edgar looked at him in surprise, the boy explained again what the assault had been all about.

The Governor was thinking again, and it seemed to him there might be a way to turn this assault to advantage after all. First, to begin convincing Juan of the necessity of his taking over the responsibility of Guerrero on his father's death. And second, to put that needed steel in Edgar's spine. So he said, "When the day comes, Juan, that you take over your country, the conditions that create men like that one there can come to an end."

Juan, frowning, looked over at the man sitting hopelessly on the tile, and the Governor could see the comprehension of responsibility growing in the boy's mind. Juan was learning to accept that responsibility; reluctantly but surely.

Juan said, dully, "I don't suppose anyone could say anything to my father."

"To make him change his ways? Hardly."

"Hardly," Juan echoed, and closed his eyes.

The Governor turned to Edgar, saying, "When that day comes, there'll be no more assassins. No more need of assassins."

Edgar understood. He nodded and said, "Amen."

Opening his eyes again, looking across at the failed assassin, Juan said, "We won't tell my father what happened. Or the police. He's just a burglar, that's all."

The Governor frowned. "Why?"

Juan turned and met the Governor's eyes. "I don't want him to go back into my father's prison. Let him go to a Mexican prison."

The Governor smiled, suddenly feeling very good. Everything would work out, and by God the boy had the stuff to be a fine leader, a fine leader. The Governor said, "That's all right. Just so he doesn't start making any speeches."

"I'll talk to him," Juan said, and got to his feet.

When the brown-uniformed policemen came trudging up the slope a few minutes later, Juan was hunkered down in front of the prisoner, talking to him in Spanish. He straightened, and came back over by the Governor, and answered the policemen's questions in English.

12

GENERAL POZOS MOVED slowly down the swaying stairway to the launch, where two sailors took his arms and helped him aboard. This was the only thing he disliked about traveling by yacht, the boarding and the leaving.

Bob Harrison came down after him, and then some other staff members. They all sat, Harrison beside the General, and the launch moved away from the yacht and turned itself toward shore.

Harrison had a pad in his lap. It was noon, and the sun was almost directly overhead, casting virtually no shadow. It was becoming hot, a little too much so, but Harrison in his gray linen suit and pale gray tie seemed cool and calm. "You will begin," he said, reading from his pad, "with a greeting from the Mayor of the city, at the dock."

"I know him," grunted the General. "He's a pig." The General was in a bad mood, not only because of the swaying stairway he had had to descend, but also because the other dark blue uniform he had changed to was far too hot for this sunny day. Within it, and all around it, the General was sweating. He was sweating rivers, sweating lakes. Everything was sticking to him.

Harrison, unruffled by the General's comment, continued to read from the pad: "The Mayor will escort you to a luncheon in your honor. The guests will be—"

General Pozos glowered silently through the reading of the list, until the name of a particular movie actress was mentioned, when he said, "Is that the blonde one?"

"No, sir. Redhead."

"Perhaps I want her."

"I believe she has just recently remarried, General, and her husband's name is on the guest list here."

"*Por nada,*" the General said, and waved a hand in a dismissing gesture. He always saved face in Spanish; he couldn't trust English to convey quite the right careless tone with which he wanted to announce that he cared nothing for the redheaded movie actress, that she was forgotten, that she did not exist. The proper nuances required his native tongue.

Harrison meanwhile carried on undisturbed, as he always did. "After lunch," he said, "which will be at the Hilton, there will be a brief news conference, and then you—"

"Reporters?" The General didn't like reporters, with good cause.

"We have guarantees of cooperation. All but two are Mexican, anyway."

"The other two?"

"One American, one British."

"I don't know which is worse." The statement wasn't irony, of which the General was incapable; it was the literal truth, announced deadpan.

"They'll cooperate, General, it's all been arranged."

"Good."

"After the news conference, you go to a suite reserved for you at the Hilton, and there you interview prospective new additions to your personal staff."

The General smiled. That meant women, and the General loved women when they were brand-new.

"From four to seven," Harrison went on, "there will be a cocktail party in your honor, given by an American author." He mentioned the name, a man whose doctor novels always made the best-seller list.

The General had never heard of him. He grunted, not caring.

"Dinner at eight," Harrison said. "The Brazilian Ambassador is the host, he has an estate outside the city."

The General didn't like Brazil, because it was so big. He pursed his lips, but kept quiet.

"You will return to your suite by eleven," Harrison finished, "and be free the rest of the evening. We leave at nine in the morning."

The General nodded. "Good," he said.

The launch, having slowed to a crawl, was reluctantly approaching the dock now, bobbing heavily in the water. Lines were thrown and fastened, the launch bumped finally against the dock, and strong hands helped the General up and onto the solid planks, where a crowd of smiling faces and poised hands waited, all in formal attire.

For the next five minutes, the General was involved in the protocol of official greetings. There was a line of faces to smile at, hands to shake, all in particular order. The General loved such fuss and ceremony just as he loved his uniforms; they made him feel good, tall, central, important.

Most of the welcoming party were politicians, of course, mayors and governors and ambassadors and so on. There was also Luke Harrison, Bob's father, and there was Doctor Edgar Fitzgerald, both men fairly far down the line. General Pozos was pleased to see them, particularly the doctor, who would be joining him here and staying with him indefinitely. He took the doctor's hand in both his own, smiling broadly. The physical troubles that had been assailing the General these past few years, particularly the increasingly frequent problem of impotence, were both infuriating and frightening. To have the care and concern of such a man as Doctor Edgar Fitzgerald was a great relief, a great relief.

The General expressed his feelings as he shook the doctor's hand, saying, "Most happy, my Doctor. Most happy. You will love your rooms on the ship, you will love them."

The doctor seemed somewhat haggard, possibly from the change of climate or diet, but he managed an answering smile and said, "I'm looking forward to seeing them, General. And to beginning—beginning our association."

"Most happy. Most happy."

The General released his hand at last, and moved on. Now he

allowed himself to be distracted while he watched young Harrison meeting his father. Would there be a clue now, a hint, the opening of a door into Harrison's interior, as he shook hands with the father he hadn't seen for nearly a year?

But it was a disappointment. The two men, father and son, shook hands and smiled at one another and murmured a few words, but so far as the General could see, it was all done with that same bland, polite good fellowship that Harrison *always* showed.

Yes, but this time there were two of them. The father acted the same way, precisely the same way, as he greeted his son. There were no broad smiles of pleasure, no bright eyes, no arms thrown around one another, no expression or gesture of blood relationship at all. But on the other hand, there was none of the stiff formality seen between relatives who have had a falling-out, either. There was nothing, nothing at all.

Was that where Harrison had learned it, from his father?

The General moved on to the next blankly smiling face, automatically outstretched hand. This a young man, Latin, slightly familiar, but with something vaguely like insolence in the eyes. The General shook his son's hand without recognition, failed to see the bitter humor that came into the boy's eyes, and moved on.

As he continued along the line, smiling, bowing his head, murmuring his words in either Spanish or English, shaking hands, he saw from the corner of his eye that the senior Harrison had stepped back from the line, was moving away from the rest. The young man with the vaguely insolent eyes moved off with him.

A minute later the younger Harrison reached the General's side and murmured, "Dad couldn't stay. He wanted to be here long enough to greet you, but now he has to hurry away. He asked me to express his apologies, and tell you he hopes to see you in Santo Stefano next month."

The General nodded. He failed to understand, but he nodded. And moved along the line, bowing and shaking hands.

Finally the initial meeting was done, this first ceremony over, and the entire party moved toward the row of limousines waiting at the other end of the dock. The General was now flanked by

Bob Harrison on one side and on the other by the Mayor of the city, who was his official host for the day. After a few paces, Harrison dropped back to make room for the Brazilian Ambassador.

They had just reached the limousines when the General's attention was caught by a disturbance far down the street. He looked in that direction, and was amazed to see two people thundering this way on horseback, rushing along as though at the steeplechase. And there were the sound of shots, and people chasing people, and great confusion, all hurtling this way.

A voice said, very loudly, "Oh, my God!" and the General was amazed to realize it was young Harrison, thrust at last out of his pale cocoon. He turned his head to see the expression on Harrison's face when all at once a fist struck him very hard on the chest, and the sun went out.

PART FOUR

WHEN THEY WENT around the first curve and could no longer see the red glow of the burning automobile back there, when there was unrelieved blackness all around them except for the light thrown off by their own car, Elly turned around in the seat, stared at Grofield's profile, and said, "What in God's name did you *do* back there?"

"Guerrilla tactics. I unhorsed them."

Grofield was feeling very good, very pleased with himself. He'd stranded that crowd so they were pretty much out of the picture for good. There would be another crowd waiting at the Acapulco end, but Grofield was feeling cocky now, certain he'd be able to take care of them, too, when the time came.

He also had a strong Richard Conte or George Raft feeling right now. Having wrecked the heavy's vehicle, he was bringing the load of oranges into Frisco on time after all, which meant the shipping contract would go to his infant company, which in turn meant Martha could get that operation on her foot. Crouched over the wheel, Grofield heard the kind of staccato background music this scene always got, and he knew the only thing missing was the cigarette dangling from a corner of his mouth.

The left corner.

He said, "Gimme a butt."

"What?"

"A cigarette. Please."

"Oh. I didn't hear you."

Grofield chuckled and settled back more comfortably in the

seat, letting the bit go. There was no point keeping your shoulders tense all the time. The background music faded, and he said, "You get some sleep if you can. Maybe I'll have you drive later on."

She handed him a lit cigarette and said, "Don't look now, but you're being noble and clever at the same time. You won't want me to drive later on and you know it."

Grofield looked at her, and back at the curving, climbing roadway. "All right," he said. "But when we get to Acapulco, you're the one in charge, you're the one who finds this General and gets us in to see him. You ought to be bright and alert for it."

"I ought to stay awake," she said, "to keep you company. You didn't have much sleep either."

"I'm doing fine," he told her. "I'm a natural driver, I could drive all night, I've done it lots of times."

"Besides," she said, "I couldn't possibly go to sleep, I'm too keyed up."

Grofield shrugged and said, "Fine by me. It's up to you."

But then she didn't say anything else, and when Grofield glanced at her again five minutes later she was sleeping, her head tilted to the side and resting against the window.

He had told her the truth about being a natural driver, about enjoying time spent at the wheel, but this highway was a strain on anyone. It curved and climbed and dipped and reversed itself, all poorly marked with signs and all in total darkness and all two lanes wide. The only item on the plus side was that there was absolutely no traffic, in either direction. Grofield kept the high beams on constantly, picking his way with wearying caution over the road, rarely able to get above thirty miles an hour. His shoulders kept tensing up despite him, until the first twinge of ache would call his attention, beginning in the area of the wound. Then he'd force himself to relax again, to sit easily and comfortably, holding the steering wheel with moderate grip. The wound had been all right the last day or so, he didn't want it to start acting up again. But soon he'd be hunched forward once more, squinting into the darkness ahead, fingers clamped around the wheel, body tense and shoulders rigid.

A man's best friend when driving alone at night is his car radio, but in these mountains there was no radio reception, and no nearby stations. Grofield tried it every once in a while and got only rasping static, which made Elly moan and shift position.

Dawn came around five-thirty, after he'd been driving two hours and had covered forty-seven miles. He was getting weary, as worn as if he'd driven ten hours, and his left shoulder ached constantly now, around the wound. He was also getting hungry, and visions of coffee danced in his head.

Driving was a bit easier in daylight, and he made better time. Half an hour later, having covered another twenty-one miles, he came to a flat section and a town, Chilpancingo. There was a big Pemex gas station on the right, with a restaurant on the second floor. Grofield pulled the car off the road and stopped next to the station.

Elly woke up as soon as the car stopped moving. She sat up bleary-eyed, saying, "Are we here?"

"No. This is a place called Chilpancingo. Rest stop."

"Oh." Rubbing her eyes with her knuckles she said, "I fell asleep."

"Sure. That's what I wanted."

"What time is it?"

"Little after six."

"My God! I slept almost three hours."

"Come on, let's go get some coffee."

They went into the rest rooms first and washed their faces, then went upstairs to the restaurant. There were no other customers this early, but three employees were already on the job. A short and serious young man perched on a stool at the cashier's desk, a heavy-set woman mopped the floor with a red rag which she pushed back and forth with a stick, and a waitress in a white uniform worked at a table in the corner, filling sugar jars.

The waitress came over as soon as Grofield and Elly settled at a table. She brought with her a smile, two glasses of water, and a pair of menus.

Grofield said, "We can't take much time, you know."

Elly nodded. "I know." She ordered melon and black coffee, and Grofield said he'd have the same.

Grofield lit a cigarette while waiting, but saw Elly's wrinkled look of distaste and put it out again. She said, "I'm sorry, it's just when I first get up."

"It's okay. It tasted bad anyway."

"I'll drive for a while, if you want."

"No. All I need is a few minutes' rest and a cup of coffee."

When the waitress came back with their order, Grofield asked her how much farther it was to Acapulco and she said, "One hundred forty kilometers."

He worked that out in his head and it came to eighty-seven and a half miles. At least another two hours at the rate they were going, and probably more. He said, "There's just the one road to Acapulco, isn't there?"

"Oh, yes."

"No other way to get there."

"Fly," she said, and smiled broadly, and pointed out the window.

Frowning, Grofield looked where she pointed and saw a couple of small airplanes in a field out there. And a runway, extending away to the right.

For just a second he considered it. Honner and the others expected them to arrive by car, so if they showed up instead by airplane . . .

No. Honner and his men must know themselves about this airfield, and in any case they wouldn't be easing up their watch anywhere, because how could they be sure Grofield wasn't working some sort of fake to throw them off guard? Besides, if he and Elly took a plane, they'd have to leave the car here, and Honner would be coming along in a while and would surely see the car and know what it meant.

So that was that. Grofield thanked the waitress and reached for his coffee.

Talking around a mouthful of melon, Elly said, "I've been thinking."

"About what?"

"The men in Acapulco. You know."

"Honner's friends."

"Yes. They won't just wait there for us, you know, at the city line. They'll come looking for us on the road, that's the best place to capture us. They'll be coming up and Honner'll be coming down, and we're in the middle drinking coffee and eating melon."

"I know," Grofield admitted. "I've been avoiding the thought, but I know that's what they'll do, they'll come for us."

"So what will *we* do?"

"You got me, honey." Grofield glanced at the planes again, standing out there with morning dew on them, and felt a longing.

"It's daytime now," she said. "You won't be able to sneak up on them this time, *or* crash by them. *Or* outrace them."

"I know, I know. Don't nag."

"Nag? That's a funny word."

"It's a funny life. You finished with the melon?"

"What are we going to *do*, Alan?"

"Think. But we'll travel while we think, it'll save time."

They paid for their breakfast and went back downstairs to the car, where Elly said, "I really ought to drive for a while. That way, you can think without being distracted."

Grofield felt it was cheating to allow himself to be talked into it this way, but his shoulder was still aching and he truly didn't want to drive, so he merely said, "It's a hell of a road, you know."

"I can drive. Give me the keys."

"Okay." He gave her the keys. They got into the car, Elly behind the wheel, and headed south again. Just past town, the road began to climb once more and to wind like a snake amid the mountains.

Grofield, on the passenger side, gazed moodily out the windshield, watching the sky turn a lighter and lighter blue, watching the cream-white hood of the Datsun turn this way and that, nosing along the corkscrew road. He wasn't getting much thinking done, but he was relaxing, and the pain in the shoulder was lessening.

All at once Elly hit the brakes hard, startling Grofield out of a reverie that was at least half nap. He looked up, expecting to see the road blocked by men with guns, and saw a whole lot of black goats instead. They were coming down a steep, overgrown hill on the left, crossing the road, and disappearing down another steep slope on the right. Two young men on horseback, wearing white shirts and trousers and dark-colored serapes and straw hats, like sombreros but with narrower brims, moved restlessly back and forth on the roadway to either side of the herd of goats, keeping them together, preventing strays.

Grofield looked at them, looked at the goats, looked at the almost invisible path the goats were following, and snapped his fingers. "Elly," he said, "if you speak Spanish, we're saved."

"High school Spanish," she said. "Why?"

"Ask them how much money they want for the horses."

"What?"

"The horses, the horses. Hurry, before they leave us here."

"But what do we want with—"

"All in good time, my darling. First, *por favor*, ask them how much for the horses."

"Well . . ."

They both got out of the car, and Elly started speaking in halting Spanish to the horseman on the near side of the herd. There was confusion for a while, and then the horseman announced that the horses were not for sale.

Grofield said, "Tell them it's American currency. One hundred dollars each for the horses, in excellent ten dollar bills."

She said it. The horseman seemed dubious, so Grofield went back to the car, opened the suitcase, got the money, and returned to show it.

The horseman was probably no more than twenty, and his partner across the road was even younger. The sight of the greenbacks impressed him, made him waver, but it wasn't enough. When Grofield saw it wasn't enough, he went back and got a hundred dollars more, and through Elly told them the price had gone up to one hundred and fifty dollars each.

The goats had stopped moving now, were baaing and bleating, stepping daintily around in the roadway. The horsemen spoke together over the goats' heads in rapid Spanish that was obviously over Elly's head as well, and then made a counter-offer. They would sell one horse, for one hundred and fifty dollars.

But Grofield shook his head. "Two horses or nothing. Tell them."

Elly told them. There was more rapid talking, some heavy thinking, and when Grofield saw that they were looking at him sidelong to see if he would go back to the car for more money, he knew the deal was set. Ostentatiously he stuffed the wad of tens back in his pocket and said loudly to Elly, "Well, it's no good. Never mind." And gestured in a way that clearly meant he was changing his mind, giving up.

Now the nearer horseman spoke to Elly again, and she reported what he had to say: "He says the saddles and blankets will have to be extra."

"Fifty dollars extra for everything."

She passed the word on, and suddenly the world was all smiles and nodding. Grofield got the rest of the money, the horsemen climbed down from their horses, and everyone shook hands all around. The horsemen, now pedestrians, got their goat herd moving again, and disappeared with the end of it over the side and down the trail and out of sight, leaving Grofield and Elly each holding a rope attached to a horse.

"Well," said Elly. "Now we own two horses. Just what I've always wanted."

Grofield swung up into the saddle while a cigarette commercial boomed about his ears. The horse was uneasy with the stranger on his back, but Grofield said, "Whoa, boy," and other appropriate things from western movies, and the animal settled down.

Grofield said, "Give me the reins of yours. Then you follow us in the car."

"And to think," she said, "I left my camera in Philadelphia."

2

THE POINT WAS, people lived here. They lived all their days and all their nights in these mountains, through which civilization had barely managed to push a single two-lane highway that squirmed and twisted and strained, threatening any moment to disappear entirely. A man in an automobile on that highway could get sloppy in his thinking, could assume that the mountains surrounding him were as inaccessible and inhospitable to everyone else as they were to him. But the truth was far different.

There were the shepherds, for instance, like the ones Grofield had bought the horses from. They lived from their small herds of goats or cattle, penning them at night in the valleys and grazing them by day in the upper slopes, now and again crossing the slender gray ribbon of tomorrow's world. And there were farmers, too; slopes that seemed too steep to walk on were under cultivation, mostly beans, the hills plowed in smooth and curving rows, exposing the black earth, so that at times the surroundings looked like a landscape in a book of children's stories, green and black, the round hills all farms.

Grofield, riding easy on one horse and leading the other while Elly followed in the Datsun, thought about how lucky he'd been to meet that goat herd and the two shepherds. Not so much because of the horses, though that was good, too, but mainly because seeing them had opened up his thinking, had made it possible for him to think of a way to avoid the people surely on their way north from Acapulco to intercept them.

But unless he found a good spot soon, they'd be intercepted

after all. They were on their way uphill now, which was promising; Grofield thudded his mount with his heels and urged him into a faster trot. Neither horse liked the pavement underfoot, so he had to keep pushing them.

At the top of this incline, where the road curved left around a bulging mass of rock, a gravel parking area had been cleared on the right, overlooking a first-rate view. Grofield didn't have time for the view right now, but the parking area pleased him. He rode past it, not wanting hoofprints on the gravel, then stopped and dismounted.

Elly had stopped behind him. She stuck her head out the window and called, "Now what?"

"Take it in on the gravel. Park it facing the rail there, and leave the motor running. No, come to think of it, turn the motor off."

"Fine." She backed up, swung around, and put the car where he'd said.

Meantime, he'd led both horses to the other side of the road and tied the reins to a bush growing out of a tiny triangle of earth between the edge of the road and the beginning of the wall of rock. Making sure they were secure, he walked back over to the car.

Elly had the door open, and said, "Should I get out?"

"You might as well, since it's going over the edge."

"It's doing what? Listen, I only *rented* this car."

"They'll take a check, don't worry. Come along."

He went over and inspected the railing at the edge. It was made of crossed posts stuck into the ground and tied together in an X shape, with a single, long, rough log lying between each pair of X's. Grofield managed to lift the end of one log out of its X, swing it outward, and drop it over the edge. The other end slid away from the X down there, and the log went bumping and rolling out of sight.

Looking over the edge, Grofield saw a long and nearly perpendicular drop, punctuated here and there by groups of trees, all leading to an indistinguishable green mass at the bottom. It was a long way down, but the cream color should show up well. Unless the car burned, of course, but with the engine off, there was less likelihood of that.

Going back to the car, he said, "In neutral, emergency brake off."

"You're really going to do it?"

"Really. We want the luggage out, too."

"I should hope so."

"We're only taking one bag each, that's all we can carry."

They spent the next few minutes rearranging their luggage. Grofield's money suitcase was barely half full of bills, so there was room for everything he wanted from the other bag. Elly, predictably, had more trouble deciding what to give up, but finally she too was ready. Grofield put the extra bags back in the car while Elly released the emergency brake and shifted into neutral, then climbed out and slammed the door, saying, "Now what?"

"Now we push."

It was just slightly uphill to the edge. They both had to lean their total weight on the back of the car before it would start rolling, and then they had a tough time keeping it in motion. But finally the front wheels rolled off the edge, and now the car was sloped somewhat downward instead.

But there were still problems. The front half of the car was no longer resting on the wheels; the body itself rested on the ground at the edge of the drop. They pushed, and pushed, and the car slid reluctantly forward, until all at once its balance shifted, they stepped hurriedly back, and the car tilted leisurely forward, like a toy. It showed its underside, like a cancan dancer, and abruptly dropped out of sight.

Grofield stepped forward, leaned over, and watched the Datsun take its last trip. The cliff was nearly vertical, but not exactly so, and the Datsun seemed almost to be running down it, one or more of its wheels touching the earth at all times. It crashed through groups of trees that Grofield had hoped might stop it and leave it more visible to eyes searching for it from above, and finally came to rest way down below, an indistinct bit of brightness in the midst of the green. Still, if Honner was looking for it, he'd surely be able to find it. Satisfied, Grofield stepped away from the edge again.

Elly, standing with arms folded, said, "Now what? We disguise ourselves as Mexicans?"

"Not a bit of it. Come here."

"You throw *me* over the edge."

"Exactly. Come here, you've got work to do."

She came over, and they both leaned on one of the remaining rails while he pointed out and ahead and slightly to the left and somewhat down and said, "Do you see the road down there? Running along, do you see it?"

"Wait. Oh, I see that stretch of rock."

"Where they blasted to let the road through. But do you see the road itself? See it? The gray, and that reddish dirt sort of stuff on each side?"

She nodded. "Yes. I see it."

"Well, you watch it. Don't take your eyes off it. That's a bit of road we haven't reached yet, and your friends from Acapulco will be coming along there very soon now, if I'm not mistaken. So if you see any sort of vehicle along there at all, you give a holler."

"Why? Where are you going to be?"

"Just down the road a bit, I'll be right back. Oh, if there is a car, it'll go from right to left."

"Of course," she said. "I'm not stupid."

"You're a dear girl."

He patted her rump, winked at her, and moved away. He crossed the road, mounted his new horse, and went riding on around the curve to see what the road did next.

What it did was head down for a fairly longish straight stretch, and then curve away and out of sight to the right. The right side of the road was a cliff all the way down, and the left side—after the mass of rock at the peak—was a steep slope upward, full of trees and underbrush.

It was this left side that Grofield watched, keeping his mount moving at a walk, and about a hundred feet down from the peak he found what he wanted; a narrow and nearly invisible trail that led in and up and out of sight. He turned the horse that way, and the animal left the highway with small, dainty steps, then stretched his legs for the first upward climb of the trail away from the road.

A few yards in, the trail angled away to the right and proceeded almost at the level, going across the prevailing slope. Already Grofield could barely see the road through the trees, and a minute later the highway had disappeared entirely. He was in a dark, silent, chilly rain forest, the trees crowded close together and the small spaces between them choked with dark green underbrush. There was practically no sunlight in here, and a moist and musky cool smell to the air. The trail Grofield rode was just wide enough for one man on horseback; if cattle were driven through here they must move one at a time.

Grofield had to keep going until he found a spot wide enough to turn around in, then headed back for the highway and up to where Elly was waiting. He dismounted and said, "Nothing showed?"

"No. Where were you?"

"In another part of the forest. Keep watching that road."

He tied the horse back with the other one, then got the two suitcases, bringing them across the road. The saddles he'd paid fifty dollars for were basic and primitive things, but they did boast extra thongs at the back. Grofield tied the suitcases on, and then went back over to where Elly was leaning on the rail and joined her there. "The way I figure it," he said, "they wouldn't have started out before sunrise, there wouldn't be any point in it. So we shouldn't expect them to show up for about half an hour yet. Still, you never know."

"What do we do when they show up? You watch the road for a while, my eyes are tired."

"Right. We hide."

"Where?"

"In the forest. In a place where no car can go. You know, those guys aren't coming to intercept two people, they're coming to intercept a car. Maybe the Datsun, maybe some other car we've switched to, maybe a truck we hitched a ride on, but in any case, an automotive vehicle of some sort. And it may occur to them that we'll try to hide and let them go by us, so they'll look everywhere along the way that a car can be taken off the road, which is almost nowhere, but they won't think to look in places where a car *can't* go."

"That's why we threw a perfectly good automobile off a cliff?"

"That's one reason. The other reason is, Honner and the people coming the other way are going to meet, somewhere along this road, and—"

Elly suddenly laughed aloud. "I'd love to see their faces!"

"No, you wouldn't. Anyway, they're going to want to know where we are. They'll look, and they'll look, and with any luck they'll see the rail missing here, and they'll look over the edge, and guess what."

She said, "We didn't make the curve?"

"That's what I'd like them to believe. Maybe they will, maybe they won't, but it's worth a try. Particularly since we don't dare leave the car up here in plain view because then they'd *know* something was up, and one of them might even all of a sudden figure it out."

"Ah. Well, good luck to us."

Grofield straightened up and stretched. After pushing the car off the edge, his back had started aching again, like a charley horse. "You watch," he said. "I've got to rest a while."

"Well, sure! I'm sorry, I should have realized—"

"Yeah yeah, but watch the road down there. I'll just sit down . . ."

Watching the road, she said, "Take a nap, if you want. I'll wake you in plenty of time."

"I don't need to nap," he said, closing his eyes against the glare. "It's just rest, a minute's rest." He leaned the good side of his back against a fencepost, and let himself relax.

All at once she was shaking his bad shoulder and saying, "Wake up! Wake up!"

The realization that he'd been asleep was the shock that woke him. He sat up, his back twinging, and said, "What? What?" He couldn't get his eyes to focus, or his mind.

"I saw a car," she said.

"Help me—help me on my feet, I'm stiff again." She helped him up, and he said, "What kind of car?"

"American, I think, I don't know what make. White."

"Could be them. Come on."

He was sore all over; it had been a mistake to stop moving, to fall asleep. Still, he made himself move, trotting across the highway to where the horses were still placidly waiting. Pulling himself with an effort into the saddle, he said, "How long was I asleep?"

"About an hour. It's almost seven-thirty now."

He led the way down the road and in along the trail he'd found before. Once they were well inside, he dismounted, none of his limbs wanting to move, and pushed past her, still mounted, heading back toward the road. "I'll see if it's them or not. Wait here, watch the horses."

He went as close to the road as he dared, and lay on his stomach there. The cool ground felt good, the cool air soothed him. He knew it wouldn't be good for long, that coolness and dampness would ultimately make his stiffness much worse, but as first aid it was fine.

He had to wait about two minutes, and then he heard the car coming up the hill. He raised up a bit, still hidden behind the screen of bushes, and got a good look at the three men in the car as it went by. The faces were all new to him, but they were in the style; they were Honner's friends, without a doubt.

As soon as they went by, he got to his feet again and hurried back to Elly. He hardly minded the stiffness, and besides, it would go away as he moved around.

"Okay, Tonto," he said, swinging back up into the saddle. "Let's ride."

3

THE SUN WAS high and bright, but here in the mountains the air was pleasant, even cool. Grofield and Elly rode along the highway at an easy lope, side by side, most of the time in silence. After nine o'clock they began to meet some morning traffic coming out of Acapulco, headed for Mexico City; mostly buses and trucks giving off black, stinking exhaust, much worse than anything in the States, but now and then some tourists in their cars, some with American license plates. California. Texas. Louisiana. One gray Chevrolet had come all the way from Maine.

The truckers and the tourists ignored the couple southbound on horseback, but the bus passengers invariably stuck their heads and arms out the windows to wave and shout and grin, probably because they had nothing to do and bus rides are so boring. Grofield, wishing he had a moustache to curl, returned the bus travelers' greeting with debonair half-salutes, feeling like a Confederate officer returning to the old plantation after the war. The background music was straight out of Stephen Foster.

Around ten-thirty, Elly said, "Slow down a minute. I want to talk to you. Before we get there."

They slowed their mounts to a trot and Grofield said, "We've got a story to get straight, is that it?"

"That's exactly it."

"With whom?"

"With everybody. And with you, too. There's one thing I haven't mentioned up till now."

He turned and looked at her, and her expression was both

sheepish and defiant. He said, "There's a boyfriend, you mean."

"Well, yes."

"Honey, you don't have to worry about me hanging around. Like I told you at the beginning, I'm married."

"That isn't the point," she said. She smiled a little, with a twist on it, and said, "I'm not so sure I wouldn't like you to hang around. But I know you won't, and what I want to say is something else."

"We never slept together."

"Yes."

"Who's going to believe that, honeybunch?"

"The important people will, if we say it right. You *can* say it right, I know you can. I hope you will."

"Who gets the performance?"

"Well, my father for one."

Grofield grinned. "I have the feeling that was just preamble. Number two is what counts."

"It isn't all that definite," she said. "We aren't married, we aren't even engaged, not really."

"Who?"

"It's just been kind of an, an understanding, that's all. For years, since we were both kids."

"Oh," said Grofield. "The Governor's son."

"Bob Harrison, yes, that's right."

"Got it," Grofield assured her. "I'll do it beautifully, you can rely implicitly on me."

"I hope so. Not that I'm completely sure in my own mind, it isn't that at all. Bob's been away so much, I hardly know him really. But he's always been sort of a stickler for propriety, so it would be better . . ."

"Don't say another word," Grofield told her. "Your secret is safe with me."

She smiled. "Thank you."

"But I want you to know," he said, leaning over to the right and squeezing her knee, "that I will never let the memory fade from my heart, of those few precious moments of bliss—"

She slapped his hand away and cried, "Don't be a stinker!" And, laughing, heeled her horse and rode on ahead.

It was just noon when they came around the last curve and saw Acapulco spread out below them like a travel poster come true. Acapulco is shaped like a huge letter C lying on its back, the letter curving around the placid water of the harbor, broad, pale, sandy beaches all along the shore, big new motels around to the left, smaller older hotels around to the right, and the tropical mumbo-jumbo white and orange calypso town in the center.

Elly pointed, crying, "That's his yacht, General Pozos' yacht! That big one, the white one, see it?"

He saw it, and as he looked at it he saw a launch move away from the yacht and slice through the water toward shore. "Here comes somebody," he said.

"Come on!!"

They were still a long way off, most of it curving and twisting and backtracking down the southern slope of this final mountain. It was another five minutes before they reached the edge of the city itself, and then there was still a long, winding descent through Acapulco's native slum, with the brown faces looking up in surprise at the gringos on horseback clattering by.

They didn't try to push their mounts faster than a trot, both because of the long four hours they'd already been ridden and because of the harsh city footing underneath.

The shaking and agitation of traveling on horseback had bothered Grofield more than he'd anticipated, making the area around his wound act up more and more. He'd finally discovered that it helped to ease the strain if he kept his left hand tucked inside his shirt, in a kind of makeshift splint arrangement, and he was riding this way now, holding the reins lightly in his right hand, lifting up and back to the rhythm of the horse's movements, the suitcase securely tied on behind.

Five minutes more and they were at the bottom of the slope, the ocean ten or twelve blocks ahead of them. There were more cars on the streets now, they were coming into an area of normal city traffic, so they went single-file down the center of the street, Grofield in the lead.

"I saw where the launch landed!" Elly called at one point. "It's to the right, to the right!"

He nodded and waved his right hand, so she'd know he'd heard her. At the end of this street there was a broad avenue going to left and right, with a grassy center divider, the avenue flanking the beaches and forming the basic C pattern of the city. Grofield turned right on this, and he and Elly rode along through all the traffic, cars and trucks and bright-colored beach buggies, approaching the dock where the launch had landed.

All at once there was a shouting to the left, and Grofield looked over there to see a bunch of them piling out of a pale blue Chrysler, all of them shouting and pointing at Grofield and Elly. And then not just pointing, but pointing guns. Shouting, "Stop! Stop!"

Grofield yelled at Elly, "Take off!" and ground his heels into his animal's rib cage. The horse leaped forward, and Elly stayed beside him, and they galloped down the center of the avenue with the sounds of shouting and shooting behind them. Grofield, twisting around to look back over his bad shoulder, saw them running along back there, saw the Chrysler making a wild U turn, thumping over the divider and heading this way.

"Yaaaaah! Yaaaaaah!" Grofield yelled into his mount's ear, lying forward so his head was almost even with the horse's, so he could see its staring eye and hear its snorting breath. "Yaaaaah! Yaaaaaaah!"

Ahead and on the left there was a line of limousines, black and pretentious, which Grofield knew had to be the place. He aimed for it, cutting across the traffic, making a beach buggy slam on its brakes with a squeal.

People were about to get into the limousines, a lot of people in uniforms or formal dress, all now turning their heads this way, staring openmouthed, while behind them men ran and the Chrysler came rushing forward and bullets were sailing through the air.

Grofield never reined in till he'd reached the first limousine, and then he yanked hard, forcing his mount to pull up short, and leaped to the ground before the animal had fully stopped. He landed off-balance, and his left hand was still stuck inside his shirt and unavailable to help, so he fell heavily, and rolled, and came up against a lot of legs. He staggered to his feet, shouting, "Elly! Elly!" and looked up to see her flying through the air toward him, openmouthed and flailing. They collided, and he went down again, and all at once he seemed to be in the middle of a forest of black-trousered legs, no opening left anywhere, and Elly was lying on top of him like a sack of wheat.

He managed to say, "Up. Up." But when she didn't move, there was nothing he could do about it. He lay there, winded, aching all over now, and gasped for breath.

The whole thing was over in a matter of seconds. The forest of legs disbanded again, there was light, there were individual voices saying surprised things in a variety of languages, and then one voice crying, "Ellen Marie! Ellen Marie!"

Now she did move, raising herself up off him, and he saw there was a streak of red on the left shoulder of her white blouse. He said, "Hey."

But the new voice was more insistent, crying her name over and over, and Grofield could see it was impossible to attract her attention. She was sitting beside him, oblivious, looking around as though hunting for something.

Grofield sat up, which cost him, and reached out to touch Elly's shoulder just as the new man finally pushed his way through and dropped to his knees in front of her. He was gray-haired, heavyset, had the look of the well-bred about him; it must be her father. The father put his hands out to touch her face, then all at once pulled back, saying, "You're hurt."

In the sea of sound all around them, they existed in a little oasis of silence. Grofield could sense it, was himself on the fringe of it. He heard distinctly her low voice saying, "Yes."

And the father again: "They shot you. They tried to kill you."

And the daughter: "That's what killing is. Don't you know?"

And then the silence was total, as they looked at one another. Grofield, on the perimeter, sat cradling his left arm and waited to see what would happen next.

What would happen next was a new wave of shouting, with a repeated name in the middle of it all: "General Pozos! General Pozos!" And then a young guy stepping into the circle of silence, ignoring it, unaware of it, putting his hand on Elly's father's shoulder and saying, "Sir, it's the General. He's been shot. Would you look, he's been shot."

The father raised his head as though befuddled, saying, "What? What? Oh, oh, yes, of course. But Ellen Marie, she's—"

She said, cold and correct, "It only cut the skin, it isn't still in me, I'm all right."

"If you—"

"I'm all right!"

The young guy—an American, in a gray business suit—said, "Sir, if you could hurry—"

"Yes. Yes, of course."

The father got to his feet first, moving clumsily, like a man who's recently had a stroke. Elly followed him, favoring her left arm but still getting up with supple grace. Grofield came last, not so gracefully, and would have lost his balance halfway up if a pop-eyed bystander hadn't given him a hand.

He looked around and the little Honners were all gone. The blue Chrysler was gone. The horses, content to be let alone at last after their long run, were still standing where Grofield and Elly had hurriedly left them.

Several people standing around Grofield were asking him questions, some in Spanish and some in English and some in other languages, but he hardly heard them and didn't acknowledge them at all. After a few seconds, in which he got himself oriented, and was sure he wouldn't fall down again, he pushed through them and followed Elly.

Here was another group, this one silent, standing in a horseshoe shape, with Elly and her father the only ones at the open end. Grofield came up behind them and looked, and a fat man in a blue uniform was lying on his back in there. Fresh blood stained and smeared the chest of the blue uniform. The fat man's eyes were closed, he was obviously unconscious, but his legs were twitching, like those of a dog who dreams of rabbits.

Grofield was the only one close enough to hear what Elly said to her father: "Save his life. *Save* it."

"But—" The father looked troubled, confused, almost pained. He made vague motions; at the fat man lying on the ground, at himself, at the world in general. "Luke—" he started, and trailed off.

She shook her head. "No. This is what you're for. You're to save lives."

A shudder went through him, and he looked panic-stricken for just an instant, like a sleepwalker awaking suddenly to foreign surroundings, and then, with an obvious effort, he regained control. "Yes," he said, possibly to Elly, possibly to himself. He turned and went to his knees beside the fat man and reached down to unbutton the jacket of the fancy uniform.

4

SOMEWHERE, SOMEONE was knocking on a door. *It must be Macbeth*, thought Grofield, *Macbeth does murder sleep*.

Reluctantly he half-opened his eyes, and saw a room shrouded in semidarkness. In that first instant he had no idea where he was, but then he shifted position and felt a sharp twinge high on the left side of his back, and remembered everything. Of course. The bullet wound, the suitcase full of money in the closet; he was in the hotel room Parker had gotten him in Mexico City.

He closed his eyes again, remembering. He'd had some sort of a wild dream, girls climbing in his window, horseback riding through mountains . . .

The room was moving.

He opened his eyes again, quickly, and it was true, it wasn't dizziness or anything like that, the room was really moving.

And the window was a porthole.

There was that knocking at the door again, but Grofield paid no attention to it. He was staring at the porthole, and loudly he said, "Hey!"

The door opened. A short steward in a white Eton jacket and black trousers came hesitantly in, saying in heavily accented English, "Good morning, sor. Is nine o'clock, sor."

Now Grofield was really awake, and had the recent past sorted out in his mind. Elly, General Pozos, Honner, all the rest of it. And here he was on General Pozos' yacht.

He sat up, aware of the fact that he was wearing yellow pajamas he couldn't remember ever having seen before. They seemed to be made of silk, and in them he felt like Ronald Colman. He said, "It's what time?"

"Nine o'clock, sor."

"At night?" But there was light outside the porthole.

"No, sor. In the morning."

"Don't be silly, we didn't get here till after noon."

"Yes, sor."

"I've taken a nap, I've . . ." He rubbed his head, trying to remember. The arrival, sailing off the horses, Elly crashing into him, General Pozos lying on the ground . . . And then the hours without sleep, and the constant activity, and the final letdown at the end, all had combined to make him suddenly sick with exhaustion. He could remember staggering to Elly, muttering something to her about the suitcase, take care of the suitcase, and then someone saying he should be in bed, and walking somewhere, and . . . and that was all.

The suitcase. He looked around the room, saying, "My—my luggage. Where's my luggage?"

"Suitcase here, sor." The steward was crossing the room to a tall dresser, picking up the suitcase from beside it. "Shall I unpack for you, sor?"

"No. No. I'll take care of it."

"Miss Fitzgerald say she in dining room, sor. Down corridor . . . that way."

"To the right."

"*Si.* Yes, sor. To the right. All the way." He opened a small door in the opposite wall, saying, "Washroom. If you want something, button here."

"Thank you. What time did you say it was?"

"Nine o'clock, sor."

"All right, then, what *day* is it?"

"Uhhhh . . . I don't know, sor, not in English. Day before Sunday."

"Saturday?"

The steward smiled brilliantly. "*Si!* Saturday!"

"Ah," said Grofield. "It's tomorrow. That explains everything."

"Yes, sor." Still smiling, the steward backed his way out of the room.

Grofield got out of bed and examined his suitcase, and all the money was still there. Good for Elly, good for her.

He took a hot shower, which helped work the stiffness out of his left shoulder, then dressed, locked the suitcase again, and went down the corridor to the right. At the end was the dining room, with large side windows through which sunlight poured blindingly. There were half a dozen tables covered with snowy cloths and sparkling plates and gleaming silver. The floor was waxed to high gloss, the metalwork around the windows had been polished till it shone, and the central light fixture in the ceiling was alive with cut glass glittering in all the light. It was something like a restaurant built inside a diamond, and Grofield didn't care for it at all.

All the tables were empty save one in the middle of the room, at which Elly sat alone. Grofield pulled his sunglasses from his shirt pocket, put them on and threaded the tables, sitting down across from Elly, who was laughing at him. He said, "What's so funny?"

"You look like a man with a hangover."

"I feel like a man with a hangover."

"I'm sorry, maybe I should have let you sleep, but I thought twenty hours was enough."

"Is that how long it was?"

"One o'clock yesterday afternoon till nine o'clock this morning."

"You always were good at math."

She laughed again and said, "You want some orange juice?"

"God, no. Coffee."

"We'll get you both." From somewhere she called up a waiter, gave him an order for a complete breakfast, and when he'd gone again, she said to Grofield, "Now, we've got to get our stories straight."

"We never slept together, we never slept together."

"I don't mean that, I mean everything else."

"What everything else?"

She leaned closer, saying, "Bob Harrison doesn't know it was his father who caused all this."

"Why not?"

"Because," she said firmly, "there's enough trouble in the world. Bob doesn't know, and I don't want him to know."

The waiter came with Grofield's coffee. When they were alone again, and Grofield had drunk half the cup, he said, "All right, it wasn't Harrison's father. What about your father? In or out?"

"Out. It's simpler that way, and Dad—"

"He reformed."

"Don't make it sound like that," she said. "It's true. When he actually saw bloodshed—"

"Hot damn," said Grofield. "I was there, I saw it, I believe it. What I don't believe is that he would have gone through with Harrison's plan in the first place."

"Oh, yes he would. I know him, and he would. There wouldn't have been any shooting, any obvious violence at all. It would have been a medical problem, an intricate medical problem. Dad would have dehumanized it. Isn't that funny? When all is said and done, violence doesn't dehumanize us but forces us to recognize the fact of our humanity."

"Gee whiz," said Grofield.

"Did anybody ever tell you you were a bastard in the morning?"

"In the morning? I don't think so. I've had people tell me in the afternoon, and at night, but never in the morning." He finished his coffee, and said, "All right, you're right and I'm sorry. What's the drill?"

"The what?"

"The new story."

"Oh. Well, there were these mysterious people who were plotting to kill General Pozos. They'd heard that Dad was going to become his personal physician, so they thought if they kidnapped me they could force Dad to help them get past the General's bodyguard."

Grofield said, "A little shaky on detail, but what the hell."

"Listen, now. They kidnapped me, and they were holding me

in Mexico City. You rescued me, because I managed to throw a note out the hotel window and you found it."

"Who am I?"

"Wait, we'll get to that. Anyway, it was Thursday night when you rescued me. I had no idea how to get in touch with Dad by then, but I knew everyone would be here in Acapulco on Friday, so I asked you to help me get here, and you did. The rest of the story is exactly the way it really happened, except that we left from Mexico City on Thursday night, and never slept anywhere, separately or together."

"I'm not sure I'd believe that story, if I were Bob Harrison," Grofield told her. "On the other hand, I've heard your stories before."

"Well, Bob believes it."

"Good for him. If he's a man you can deceive, I'm sure you'll be very happy with him, forever and ever."

"What's that supposed to mean?"

"Nothing, darling. Let's get back to me. Who am I?"

"I'm not sure. You're also mysterious. I do know you've had a recent bullet wound, and I know you're in Mexico without papers."

"Do you know my financial condition?"

"The money? No, of course not. The impression I've given Bob is that you're some sort of adventurer, but basically a good man. He wants to talk to you later."

"A lot more than I want to talk to him, I bet."

"He'll arrange some sort of—here he comes."

"What?" Grofield looked up to see the waiter bringing his breakfast on a tray. From the opposite direction, Bob Harrison was coming across the room, smiling in a genial way. Arriving, he said, "Good morning. I'll have a cup of coffee with you, if I may."

"Sure. I'd like another myself."

Harrison sat down, saying, "The General's resting easy." He reached out and put his hand on Elly's, saying, "Your father's been wonderful, Ellen, absolutely wonderful."

"He's the best there is."

"He's taking a nap now, maybe he'll join us later."

Grofield said, "He's here? On the ship?"

Elly told him, "We're all here. There's a regular infirmary here. It was closer than anything else, so the General was brought here right away yesterday."

Harrison said, "It was also more convenient. As soon as Ellen's father says it's safe, we'll be returning to Guerrero so the General can recuperate in his own land."

"He'll be all right, then," said Grofield.

"Yes." Harrison's smile, so affable and impersonal, faded all at once, and he seemed to be looking back at yesterday. "God, that was something," he said. "When the General fell, I thought they'd—I thought he was dead." He lifted a hand to his face; the hand was shaking. "I thought they'd killed him."

Elly, looking concerned, reached out to touch his arm, saying, "Bob? What's the matter? I've never seen you this way."

Harrison's hand covered his face now, and his voice was muffled by it when he spoke. "God, I love that man," he said. "You don't know what it did to me, when I thought he was dead." Emotion made his voice fluttery and uncertain. He lowered his hand and turned toward Grofield a face reddened and puffed by the violence of his feeling. "All that vitality," he said, "all that strength, all that great love of life, just *lying* there!"

Grofield couldn't resist it, couldn't keep himself from saying, "The way I hear it, there are people who'd like to see General Pozos just lying there, for good and all."

"Peasants! *Little* people, *nobodies, cowards,* all the *gray* little people who never *lived!* They say he's a dictator, he's a tyrant, you'll even hear atrocity stories if you go looking for them, but so *what!* Some men are just bigger than others, that's all, more alive, more vital, more *important!* You can't stop them, you can't contain them, hold them in with rules! Ellen understands that, don't you, darling, you risked your own life to try to save him, you sensed the drive in the man, the force, the power."

Elly was startled out of any ready answer. "Well," she said. "Well. I just did, I only did . . ."

"You know what I say?" Harrison turned to stare at Grofield, his hands clutching the edge of the table. "I say, if a hundred men starve themselves to death in darkness in order to produce one after-dinner cigar for General Pozos to enjoy on just one evening of his life, those hundred men have fulfilled their purpose! What *else* would they do with their lives, what *more* meaningful than devote themselves to the pleasure of one of the few men who are really and truly alive? The people of Guerrero should be *proud* to have General Pozos for their leader!"

Grofield said, "I understand your own father is a different kind of leader, has maybe a different attitude toward people."

"Oh, all that. I grew up with that, I know about that. I think it's all very praiseworthy, I'm sure my father did the people of Pennsylvania proud, I'm not saying there's anything wrong with being an administrator. But General Pozos— He's so far above that paperwork bureaucrat sort of thing, he's so— He's a lion in a jungle full of rabbits."

Elly, straining to change the subject, said, "Your father went back north, didn't he?"

"Oh, yes. He had appointments, he only stayed long enough to be sure the General was going to be all right, then he flew on home. He and Juan." Turning to Grofield, he explained, "The General's son."

"Ah."

"The oddest thing," Harrison said. "Someone tried to kill Juan today, too. Some lunatic, I suppose. Just ran up to him at the hotel and tried to stab him."

Grofield looked at Elly, but she shook her head, meaning it was news to her and didn't have any connection with the rest of it that she knew about. Grofield said to Harrison, "Was it the same mob, you suppose? Trying to kill the father and the son both on the same day?"

"The Mexican police are looking into it," Harrison said, "but it doesn't seem likely. More probably a dope addict, something like that. The General's the one the gang was after. I don't want to say anything against Juan, I'm sure he's a pleasant boy, but he has none of his father's power, his electricity. No, it was the General they wanted."

"I suppose so," said Elly faintly.

"Everyone can sense that power in the General, that aura. My father, too, he can feel it, he missed his plane to stay here and be sure the General was going to be all right."

"Good of him," said Grofield, looking ironically at Elly.

All at once, Harrison sat back in his chair and offered them a sheepish smile, saying, "I'm sorry, I don't usually carry on like this. But it was such a shock, I don't think I'm over it yet."

Elly said, "You were going to see about papers for Mister Grofield."

"Oh, yes." Harrison was making an obvious effort to settle down. Trying for his usual affable smile, he said to Grofield, "Ellen tells me you're something of a mystery man, traveling around with bullet wounds instead of papers. Well, we can get you fixed up. I can have papers for you in an hour, good enough to get you safely back into the States. Or, if you like, you could come along on the rest of the cruise, be the General's guest in Guerrero for a while, I'm sure he'd like to thank you personally for your aid in defeating the plot against him."

"I think," Grofield said, "I think I'd rather leave today. I've got people I'm supposed to see in the States."

"Certainly. No problem at all."

Elly said, "Mister Grofield, would you mind if I traveled with you? I have to go north right away myself."

Harrison said, "I thought you were coming along with us."

"No, I have all sorts of responsibilities back in Philadelphia. Until I was kidnapped, I didn't know I was coming down here at all."

"What a shame," said Harrison. He smiled brightly at both of them and said, "Well, at least you'll have a more pleasant travel companion on the way back."

Elly smiled at Grofield. "Isn't that lucky," she said.

Getting to his feet, Harrison said, "Well, let me see about that paperwork for you. I'll talk to you a little later."

Grofield smiled back at him. "Fine," he said. He kept smiling until Harrison was gone, then looked at Elly and said, "What's up?"

"The balloon. All these years Bob's been the strong, silent type, that's what mostly attracted me about him. Thank God he finally opened his mouth before I married him."

"Speaking of married," Grofield reminded her, "I still am."

She shook her head. "Not till we cross the border," she said.